# STRAWBERRY FIELDS

*HILARY PLUM*

Cover image by Juliet Goodman
11.6 x 15.9 inches at 300 dpi

Published in the United States by Fence Books
Science Library, 320
University at Albany
1400 Washington Avenue
Albany, NY 12222

www.fenceportal.org

This book was printed by Versa Press
and distributed by Small Press Distribution
and Consortium Book Sales and Distribution.

Library of Congress Control Number: 2018934073

ISBN 13: 978-1-94-438003-8

FIRST EDITION
10 9 8 7 6 5 4 3 2

This is a work of fiction. Any resemblance to actual persons (living or dead), businesses, or events is coincidental. If this work refers to historical events and figures, it is in a fictitious manner; the references and narratives in the pages that follow are products of the author's imagination and not to be mistaken for fact.

## THE FENCE MODERN PRIZE IN PROSE

**Hilary Plum,** *Strawberry Fields*
**Ottessa Moshfegh,** *McGlue*

# STRAWBERRY FIELDS

*HILARY PLUM*
**FENCE MODERN PRIZE IN PROSE**

FENCE BOOKS

Yet through the country of
My eyes had no color but what they saw

**ZACH SAVICH**

All I was holding was a chocolate bar and
a cigarette when they opened fire on us.

**PROTESTOR, 2011**

to ZACH

*T*he children's suffering has been unimaginable. Many escaped from the militias under threat of death, walked sometimes hundreds of miles, often pursued, to refugee camps. Others were found in the front of the ranks when the militias surrendered or were overtaken. On liberation they entered a years-long system of refugee camp after camp, endless bureaucratized attempts to locate their families, intermittent efforts at therapy, and lengthy applications for ultimate relocation, most of their villages gone. We conducted our interviews primarily at the refugee camps. For many it was their second or third camp, and what they were most concerned about was finding their families, often one sibling in particular, whom they asked us about repeatedly, hoping we could help or believing that's why we were there. We're journalists, we told them, though we'll try to help, and we told them the names of our news services or home countries, in which they showed no interest. Our interpreters were almost always child soldiers, now employed by NGOs, and we didn't know how accurate their translations were. I believe now that sometimes we pursued only the inquiries of the interpreter. One, whom I will call Tamim, often cried, and refused to speak to many of the children.

Some of the children we could speak to directly because they had learned English or French, usually the English from missionaries, we concluded from their vocabulary and the tone of their replies. A few spoke English, however, with profoundly sophisticated grammar and sentence structure, and this was how we learned of the schoolmistress. Were you in school? we asked, unbelieving. Of course, the children said, school, every day we weren't fighting. One boy borrowed our clipboard and drew a map of his native country, complete with the dotted lines negotiated in the last peace process. Next to it he copied out a list of names from memory, his script elegant despite his wounded right side (he walked with an awful limp): the names of his own militia's leaders, and the charges already brought against them in the international courts, and then, in a separate list, the names of the president and his cabinet, their party affiliations and the dates they ascended to power, and, in some cases, their pending indictments as well. The school was here, he said, placing a dot on the map. Where is the village where you were born? we asked. I don't know, he said, seeming upset that after all this we'd posed a question he could not answer correctly. We apologized and thanked him. Do you want to know who captured us, another boy said, we know those names too. This boy had been standing to the side silently, as he often was; a machete scar split his lip and he was hard to understand. The others called him by the name of a local bird because he could often be heard whistling, which his disfigured lip made him wildly good at, able to sustain two tones at once. He took the clipboard and wrote out three names of rebel leaders and seven names of villages. We believe they return here regularly for supplies, he said, all at once as though in recitation. In at least one case we knew he was correct. Who taught you this? we asked. They told us her name, which meant in

2

their language, the beautiful one. Was she very beautiful? the Argentine human rights reporter asked. They shook their heads, laughing. Is she alive? we asked. They didn't know. Later we learned that these very children had been through one of those seven villages and burned it, all the crops, dozens of villagers dead. One hut had been left standing, abandoned by the time the government forces came. I tried to find the boys again to see if they would say more, at the least who had led the attack. But by this time, only a week later, a new influx of refugees had arrived, and it was hard to find anyone in the camp. We journalists went nowhere without word traveling before us. As, where I'm from, it's said you can tell from the birds whenever a bear moves through the forest, even distantly; at least this is what my grandfather would tell me, slowly pointing.

We turned in copies of everything the boys reported to the camp administrators and representatives of the appropriate NGOs. Some just nodded, seeming to have seen this material before, and others, without taking our names or examining the documents, insisted they had already notified the military of every lead. What do you know of this school they attended? we asked. It's not the first we've heard of it, Ellen, our favorite camp administrator, said. Who is the teacher? we asked. Ellen shook her head. You don't think they made her up, the shorter Swedish radio journalist said. No, Ellen said, but children are easy to fool.

I traveled all night and it was 4:30 in the morning when I arrived at the hospital.

Modigliani was standing outside the main entrance, behind him the yellow light of the hospital door, which gave his skin a distinct sheen and he was more radiant than I'd ever seen him. You look well, I said, and, not knowing whether to embrace him, extended a hand. Sure, last time I saw you, he said, we'd been living in that trailer for what, a month after the hurricane. There was no water, he said, as if satisfied to remember this detail, though the hurricane had been memorable and only five years had passed. It smelled like burned tires all the time, I said, all the way to the horizon, and nothing was ever dry.

Come with me, he said, his hand on my shoulder and he turned toward the yellow glow, the doors sliding open before us.

We passed through a long waiting room, where one teenage kid sat, arm wrapped in a towel, the TV in the corner rebroadcasting the senator's resignation speech. In the halls there were orderlies, men who must have been patients, but no one greeted us, not a nod. I called you because I can trust you, Modigliani said, walking slower than I expected. It's hard to know what inspires trust. He may have read my articles about the hurricane, his investigation, but if he had he never said. I think it was a volume of disquiet that we may have shared, or that we associated with one another. Together five years ago in the morgue where the highest number of flood-reclaimed bodies had been taken we'd discovered the fact of the shootings.

I can't exaggerate our discomposure, in the smell in that room, realizing that this man and this woman had not died of the water that left them now unrecognizable. The water from which they'd been retrieved with such tenacity and collective outcry, and which in receding seemed to have dulled the sky. Modigliani had in astonishment pushed at the bullet wound in the back of the head with his rubber-gloved finger, the young woman technician had cried out at him. In the last article in my series, published almost four years ago, I had noted with more than appropriate scorn that the investigation, which he had headed, was still open. There were rumors that something was in the hands of the state attorney general, but nothing has ever come of it, and I haven't followed up. I have never wanted to return to that city.

I'm going to tell you what you can talk about and what you can't, Modigliani said, opening a door into what looked like a residential wing, wood paneling ceiling to floor. I waited for him to elaborate, but he didn't, and I remembered that this, waiting for him to go on, was just what it had been like those months. The scene was now before us, at the end of this hallway, the usual sinister crowd of police and forensic workadays and photographers, yellow tape, nurses lingering, bringing coffee, usually, in my experience, in order to try to tell people what to do. The rooms where the crimes had occurred were down a small corridor to the right. Modigliani lifted the tape for me to duck under, at the same time tucking my press pass between the buttons of my blouse, the *A* of *Alice* the last letter to disappear. Five victims, he said, four men and one woman. But he'd said that already on the phone.

The scenes I saw were more terrible than the photos that were to become ineluctable, and so those have always looked staged to me, somehow bowdlerized. They only released the photos taken after the bodies had been removed, so that in every newspaper you saw only blood, sheets twisted toward the floor as though to signify that the sleeper had been hauled out, thrown to the wall, drops of blood tossed everywhere over the small room, and one bright smear—bright when I saw it, darkened by the time the dailies' photographers were permitted, what had been the body replaced by a tape sketch, almost unseeable.

I saw too how the pages of a book had been torn out and laid across not the faces but the shoulders or breast, only some of the pages bloodied, the rest thin and delicate and still lifting and settling slightly with the movements of those of us in the room. A mass-market edition of a substantial volume, I thought, and said, It's the Qur'an, in English. One of the forensics turned toward me and said, How did you know that?

I recognize that edition, I said, I used to read it in a hotel room in nowhere, Turkey, I was on assignment, Black Sea oil thing—I mean, I brought it there myself, it wasn't the hotel's—I continued to explain, although no one was interested: perhaps this impulse was what Modigliani trusted in me. I looked at him, but he was talking again to the coroner.

They were all vets of Iraq, Modigliani said, turning back toward me and gesturing me out of the room: A sniper, an infantryman, an MP, a bomb guy, and I don't know what the other one was, he seems to have been some sort of liaison with the local forces, something like that, he was mostly in Basra. In here, he said, having maneuvered us through the crowded hallway to the next open door.

Someone had pulled a sheet over the body, the woman, I learned, so that beneath the pages this time was a pale green cloth, reddened, a human form, but more peaceful, the bed beside it stripped bare. She was like that, he said. He said, If you want, I could tell you why I'm here, I mean, why I got called in.

Later, I said.

He said, Some guy upstairs saw two men running through the intersection down this hill—he pointed out the window—in the dark, he doesn't know when. The guy can see the traffic light at the entrance and he heard brakes, then saw two men wearing black running through the intersection, he says. It's a long ways off. We'll look for the driver who stopped but don't expect much. No one else heard anything, so we're assuming they used silencers, but the guys here are pretty drugged up at night, most of them we couldn't even wake up enough to interview, and the nurses said we had to wait and were starting to wave clipboards, which I'm sure you can talk to them about and they'll invoke confidentiality.

By now we were standing in the doorway of the third room, looking right at each other so as not to have to look into it. Although in this case the body was nearly obscured by the open closet door and an overturned chair. There's this doctor here, a woman, who's running a PTSD study, Modigliani said, these five were all her patients. You can interview her later today, she was too upset to talk to—I said to her, well, at least it's not suicides.

I shouldn't have said that, he added, but we're all human.

He said, You can print that they all served over there, and someone shot them, but we don't know how they were connected and we won't discuss our leads. In a few more hours you can probably just use their names. He was looking at me as though he expected me to write this down, but whenever I'm at a scene I keep my hands in my pockets. It seems like that's just the truth, I said. Modigliani nodded.

The girls wanted cigarettes and magazines. I was told to bring nothing; the doctors were quite clear. Come on, I said to the orderly who saw me slipping this contraband out from under my too-big black smock, the girls surrounding me, their hands a grasping arrangement of bones. She frowned. I dressed now under the influence of the girls, everything too big for me. Tunics and flowing pants that a drawstring hardly secured. Pulled my hair back, bright lipstick. The girls were not fooled, anyone could see I wasn't one of them. My tunic didn't hang square and wide but hugged my breasts, my pant legs taut with muscle and flesh, how I filled every chair. Even my hands were unlike theirs, when I pushed my phone across the table between us, my arm, slim as it was, had a softness.

Tell me why you're here. I pressed record.

Some shrugged, some looked at me scornfully. Some, like M, told whole life stories: teen rebellion, heroin, sex, a band I was surprised anyone could have taken so seriously, the clichéd reactions of Mom and Dad, *and then*—her hands thrown wide to encompass the tasteful institutional room, the sounds of television and whir of the one feeding-tubed girl in her purgatory in the corner—*and then they sent me here. To recover.* With this last phrase she made air quotes, twin twitch of her red-polished nails, and snapped her gum. Her breath was foul.

This is my boyfriend, one girl said—I call her L, very

11

gentle—and showed me a photo. In the photograph her face was still rounded like the child she was, she looked bobble-headed, her hand pressed to a boy's chest and hips turned toward his in a pose normal enough but which her frail body made look obscene. He was regular-looking, frosted hair, graphic T-shirt, athletic shorts. To make her shorts shorter she'd rolled the waist into a thick rope that sat low on her hips. You guys look so cute, I said. Does he come to visit? It was too far for visits, a five-hour flight from her home to the center. The girls came here from all over the country—after treating that one teen pop queen the center had received so much attention, its star in ascendance (as I myself had written), that the waiting list for admittance was now well over a year long. Exceptions possible for those in medical crisis. Unlike other treatment programs, the director had told me, we radically remove women from the family environment.

In the leisure room I surveyed the girls playing cards, sharing earbuds, watching TV (the center's own channel, expurgated of negative imagery), or even—though many were old enough to vote, go to college, have families of their own—coloring quietly, trading pencils that one girl took it upon herself each morning to sharpen. The girls bickered and were in moments, I knew, very cruel. But seeing them it was natural to think that they must somehow have birthed one another, emerged together from a mythic sea, surf and light gracing their spectral forms, salt glistening in the hair that furred their limbs. All my girls stay in touch, one of the psychiatrists had told me, gesturing to the postcards and snapshots that crowded a bulletin board behind her. Skinny women sitting implausibly in front of birthday cakes; a small girl embracing a dog; two perfectly normal women at the beach, in over-sized sunglasses and matching orange-and-white-flow-ered bikinis, a roll of flesh perched atop the elastic of the bottoms, and I searched their faces for a hint of which one might once have been here, in a body now abandoned, disappeared. Thirty to forty percent recovery rate is the norm, the psychiatrist said, we hope to improve on that drastically, and so far our results are encouraging. But it's too soon, of course, to say.

I toured the grounds, the riding stables and ring, the vegetable garden, a field of badminton nets billow-ing. There's no pool and that's deliberate, my guide, Dr. Harrison, said. Harrison treated the medically urgent cases, those patients who were transferred here directly from hospitalization elsewhere; the center had five fully equipped rooms. Several of the girls you've met came to us in that condition, he said. Two young girls with half-braid-ed hair, knees large as apples, walked past us, lugging be-tween them a bucket of carrots presumably meant for the horses. The two youngest, Harrison said, they get along well.

At all the centers I'd been to thus far I'd observed mealtimes. The girls lifting fork to mouth, fork to mouth, not looking at one another, or talking too much and too brightly, fingers fussing their food into heaps and crumbs. I watched the staff watch them, documented the forms and styles of their interventions: sitting next to the girls and counting bites, or simply walking down the rows and placing both hands on a set of shoulders in silence. Here my request to sit in at a meal had been refused. We take a strict disciplinary approach, I was told, and employ inno-vative therapeutic procedures. I'm sorry. The girls told me little more. I was provided several weeks' worth of menus and their nutritional values, as well as the CVs of every worker involved in meal planning. But no more, not even a sample meal of my own. I returned to my interviews, determined to speak to every girl. This afternoon like every other as soon as I sat down J brought me a cup of coffee, two Sweet'n Lows. I like your bracelet, B said, her fingers on the filigreed silver. The girls were always touching one another, the orderlies, even me. Just to cross the room they threaded their wrists through one another's elbows, they walked down the hall to mealtimes holding hands. When the feeding tube broke out in its wretched beeping, a girl sprang up to rub its blockage clear, the girl to whom it was attached murmuring a thank you from her doze on the couch. B's fingers were cold on my wrist, her clavicle a pool of shadow dark enough to hide a coin in. Thank you, I said, touching the bracelet myself—It was my grandmother's.

Really? All my grandmother's jewelry is so ugly, T said, from where she was sitting at the far end of the table, playing solitaire and listening in. Oh, mine too, I said, this was in a box of things she never wore.

# DANIEL

*I*n those days the story everyone wanted was the story of the mistress shared by the General and his son, but no one had anything. Once a week or so, an editor or all-around no one at whatever service would ask, or I'd get a furious text message claiming that someone else had a scoop, get on it, that someone had seen her getting into a car in one of the old bourgeois neighborhoods or leaving a resort in Switzerland or the Sudan. None of this ever panned out. Do they even have resorts in the Sudan? we'd ask in the basement the hotel manager had given over to us, after a photographer had been shot on the balcony two years ago, the glint of his lens catching the eye of a tank gunman, the tank gun swiveled so quickly, everyone who had seen it said. One maid had been deafened. So we hunkered down belowground, our sat phones in competition, calls getting through in slow motion, so it seemed, in the corner our tower of beer cans like a monument to the teetering West. I was in Sudan for two years, one guy said, Khartoum. I have often forgotten that about myself, he added—It was after the embassy bombings, but you have no idea how little happened after that.

We were all hounded about the mistress and we sympathized with one another, but we all wanted her, we tried everything stupid. Charlie—who was Vietnamese and had chosen this nickname for himself when he got his doctorate in Moscow, he explained to the Americans, who

15

found other ways to address him with a desperation that I think was his one true pleasure—had what we agreed was the worst story. Following a lead he had gone out to one of the old Jewish neighborhoods, neighborhoods none of the present-day residents would refer to this way. He'd heard that a man lived there who had been a handler of sorts for the mistress, had escorted her to the General's stronghold up north, the one rumored to have had the most opulent bedroom of them all, though there was no way to verify even this, it had been stripped bare after the overthrow. But the man had turned out to be no one—a former football player, Charlie said, now blind in one eye. The man said he knew nothing, sometimes there was a woman at the games who was said to be her, but no one had ever known anything. The son of the General had earned international notoriety for his torture of the football team after they had for the third year in a row failed to make even the regional championships. Which admittedly had been a real disappointment to many. Charlie said the man cursed him and shouted him out of the house, the man's children trailed him down the street waving pipes and shouting slurs that Charlie, with his proficiency in languages, translated for our benefit.

We spent a long time that night experimenting to see how much the loss of an eye might affect one's game, taking turns shooting goals at the beer can tower until the ball, which had been soft at the start, was limp and disc-like. It was a serious disability, we determined, but certain head movements could nearly compensate.

I learned all I was to learn of the mistress six months later, when the inquiries had dwindled, the son hanged. By then I had rented a room not far from the hotel. The hotel had since rented out a large block to subcontractors' fixers, men who were essentially hustlers but answered to no one, they claimed, and brought in whore after whore at night, no old-fashioned discretion, despite the lobby's still intact chandelier and ornate balustrades. Half the girls were barefoot and from the basement we could hear too much. I left, as did most of the journalists, though a few of the old diehards stuck it out, as though to insist that there was no experience they wouldn't have in this country.

My new landlady lived by herself. The rooms were clean and the neighborhood almost quiet and my time there was on the whole the most peaceful I had those years. The house had a garden, bare but shaded, and the story between my rooms and the landlady's remained unoccupied.

The landlady and I rarely spoke—it was clear she thought sociability with a young foreign man like myself would be inappropriate—and often only her scent in the stairwell or the nearly indiscernible murmur of the radio betrayed the fact of her presence. But one day I interrupted her on the terrace. I had left my bag there, having gotten a phone call mid-smoke and needing to run up to my computer to dispute some idiotic line edit. When I came back down an hour later, she was sitting at the table and looking at my passport, holding it close to her face.

Picture's dreadful, I tried to joke, and of course the name is a fake.

She looked at me and arched her eyebrows. She said, The name is yours, and she tossed the passport down onto the table, not replacing it in my bag's inner pocket as I had expected.

She said, It's a bit cheaply done, for such a rich country. I said, I had no idea.

I stood for a moment, meaning to gather my things and go in, but that too seemed impolite.

She gestured me toward the chair across from her and I sat; she poured half the contents of her tea cup into the cup I'd left on the table. I offered her a cigarette, which she lit with matches that had been tucked into the corner of her tea tray.

I used to make glue, she said. She laughed at my look of surprise, a squawking laugh that shook the vacant twigs of the lemon tree above us. She said, Glue for passports, and tapped mine lightly, pushed it back toward me.

She said, My husband worked in the passport and visa office, and so it was a sort of favor, or useful thing to do. During the bad years people would come in, important people, businessmen or dignitaries, and they'd all be shouting about their passports, how their passports were falling apart though they were brand new, the photos peeling off, they would never last, on and on. We couldn't use the good glue because of the sanctions. There was some ingredient in it. I don't know how that worked. But I started making some glue, homemade, you know. It took a few tries and then it was very good.

She looked at me, tucked her scarf back around her hair, away from her cigarette.

Then, of course, you make it on the side, and you're very good, everyone comes to you. Everyone wants to get out of the country, but they can't get a fake passport, not with the right glue, it turned out to be sort of special, particular. I know these things do not seem important. But it was very brittle, so that the pictures would all start to crack a little in the same way, and could not be peeled off, but you could see the small cracks in them. I'm sure you cannot imagine. So I started doing this for the black market, which paid much more. I sent whole families out of my country, they paid me in old jewelry, cash, deeds to tracts of land in the south, and there I was, taking it all, holding their babies as they counted out the fee, singing little songs to shush them.

She ashed her cigarette and I opened my passport to its photo, closed it when she resumed: The fighters came too, very suspicious, they would deal only with me, and every time they came they would tie my husband up and gag him, it was terrible. We think this very much added to the strain on his heart. I made them what they wanted. They came here from all over the world and now they live among us with nice family names.

Do you still—?

She shook her head.

I stopped once the occupiers arrived, I didn't want to be caught. But the whore came to me then, in those last days. You know who I mean, yes—she waved a finger at me, nearly smiling—the one they say the father and the son both had, kept in the palace they built after the massacre of the northern villages. The whore was there, sitting in my basement, a neat pile of cash and a European visa prepared, very hard to get. She was very young. This is what you thought when you saw her, not that she was beautiful, but that she had the sort of face, very far-apart eyes, that you could rely on to look like the face of a woman who had had no experiences. The strange thing is— this was after I sent my children and my family abroad, meaning to follow them, but then my husband died and

I had to tend to his affairs and to his people alone—the strange thing is that her real name, or the name on her passport, was the same name I had used on my daughter's. Either the same fake name, or we had chosen for my daughter a name which was truly the whore's. The whore, the one in the sunglasses, the infamous one!

I said to the whore, you have the same name as my daughter, and she nodded, though of course this was not something she could have known. Nor should I have said anything, surely her guard could have struck me. I worked tenderly and well on her passport for this reason, and because—this you will not believe—because she and my eldest daughter, they also wore the same perfume.

She leaned forward to brush ash and leaves off the table.

What visa? I asked.

She shook her head and smiled.

When I told this story to Charlie he clapped me on the shoulder and shook his head. He was neither discreet nor indiscreet, and if there had been more of a story, I'm sure he'd have told it widely and as though it had happened to him. But I don't think he did. By then in that city even the journalists were dying at unprecedented rates, which seemed to multiply the stories that circulated among us, and often you felt that your work could never end.

# ALICE

*I* didn't see Modigliani for a few days, then we met for coffee, if you could call it that. He didn't call, just turned up outside my hotel, coffees in hand. I remembered you like to stop home to clean up about now, he said, which was true, that's what I like: just before dinner, wherever home was. Come on, he said, gesturing with the cup, let's walk.

Modigliani was wearing a T-shirt and jeans and the undersides of his arms were so pale they were almost bright. That city was too sunny, wouldn't cool off until late.

The coffee was black, the only way I drink it.

We walked around the corner and said nothing until we reached the park a few blocks over, sat at one of the picnic tables, and soon enough the young mother on the far end got up and left. With one finger beneath my sunglasses I rubbed at the mascara I knew must have bled in the heat.

How's it going? I said.

He shook his head.

Off the record? I said.

He said: Even less.

Chatter on the airwaves? I said, pushing my sunglasses onto the top of my head.

Modigliani smiled, which only emphasized the fragility of the skin beneath his eyes. None of us were as young as we'd been after the hurricane. Nothing useful, he said, not one damn thing.

Are we talking domestic or foreign? I said.

He looked over my shoulder, where a couple boys had arranged themselves by the entrance to the park, do-rags darkening with sweat.

You look tired, Modigliani said.

I went to see one of the widows today, I said. Kareem's wife, Simone. Did you know they moved here—I gestured around us, although she lived in a very different part of town—just for the veterans' hospital? They sold her family place and moved across the country. Their condo is unfinished. I guess he was supposed to do all the handy stuff and now she's a wreck, there are paint cans and rolls of tiling all over and the shower's not caulked. She was wearing a huge paint-stained sweatshirt but these boots with stiletto heels.

You've probably met her, I said.

Modigliani nodded, noncommittal.

I went on: She said that he was tall and she's short, so she always wore heels. She asked me if I wanted to see the nursery. The baby is nine months old and Kareem couldn't be trusted with him, anxiety attacks, all the time. The nursery—I looked at Modigliani, eyebrows raised, and he shook his head—has a menagerie theme, that's what she called it. Bears on balls, unicorn, flowers with huge round-cheeked faces, a chimera with this sparkling mane. Glitter in the paint, Simone said, which she'd mixed in herself. She needed a project, she said, because she wasn't working and she's always worked. The nursery walls weren't finished, on the fourth there were only tape outlines, the next batch of animals. The animals were very well done, if you looked at them individually, but altogether the room was a nightmare.

She told me that she tried to get Kareem interested in it, in the nursery, but he wasn't. Not because he was sick, just that it wasn't ever his kind of thing. I asked about Kareem staying nights at the hospital. She said it was temporary, a stage in his treatment, just a few days. Which isn't what the PTSD doctor had said, but I think that's a normal sort of incongruity.

Modigliani was rubbing a hand over his stubble.

I think she's been sawing off her boot heels, I said. I saw them in the trash in the kitchen, six or eight boot heels, it took me a sec to figure out what they were.

The coffee was still too hot to drink. It was dinnertime and the last two mothers in the park were leaning against the swing set, chatting and ignoring the teens, one toddler on a swing, one wrapped around her mother's leg, mother's hand fiddling with the girl's hair.

No one on the next flights out was of interest, Modigliani said, everyone's still on alert but hopes aren't high. No descriptions, he said, we don't know if they drove, flew, or swam away. He looked at me with an air much like frankness. The bullets revealed nothing, the reconstruction established what anyone would have thought: two experienced shooters, moving fast. So far no group has claimed any kind of responsibility, he said, in fact, in the usual places no one's even talking about it, at most an offhand mention, like someone just reading the news.

Take this, he said, and gave me a card, contact info for a recruiter at Xenith, the private military company that two of the victims had signed with after their tours ended. But I had this info already.

I have to go, he said, though he only looked at his phone after he said it, then added, I'll walk you back.

I stopped at the corner store for chocolate milk and a magazine. Modigliani took his leave at the front of my hotel, which was quiet, no one coming or going, the revolving door tinged orange by the lowering sun. He took a keychain out of his pocket and clicked it vaguely at the lot, as though needing the beep to determine which car was his.

I'm going to look at my notes and make some calls, take a bath, I said, though he hadn't asked.

Get some sleep, he said, and rested his hand on my shoulder again, a gesture he must have acquired in recent years. He smiled suddenly, then he walked to his car. I remembered a night in the trailer we'd shared after the hurricane: he had come in late, so late it was morning. By then we rarely traveled together, both deep in the investigation; if I tried to tail him he called me out. That morning I was lying on my bunk in the corner, light coming through the thin blanket hung over the window. I was touching myself and had been for a while, not even wanting a climax, just to pass the time until I had to get up. I didn't know Modigliani was there and how could he not have seen my wrist's rhythm shifting the sheet? I looked up and there he was. He had what you might call no expression. Get some sleep, I said to him and rolled over, my hand beneath me, invisible.

*When was your most recent sighting of the Kind cat, and what evidence are you prepared to present of the Kind cat's existence?*

Kind.

*I'm sorry?*

Not kind, Kind. Note the short I. German for child.

*Ah yes, thank you. When, then, was your most recent sighting of the Kind cat?*

Ten months ago, about forty kilometers northwest of here, in the forest, not far outside one of the little towns along the old railway. She was burying a kill, a small deer. It is very rare to see this. I was at a great distance, so as not to disturb her. I returned to the kill, of course, numerous times over the next week, but I did not see her again. The kill was soon scavenged by foxes and the like, which perhaps she knew and is why she abandoned it.

*But neither this nor any of your previous sightings have been confirmed by other scientists, or by physical evidence of any kind?*

Kind.

*Sorry?*

No, no, a little joke. No, it has not been confirmed, but no one else cares, so who would confirm it? They do not know anything and would dismiss my bite mark analyses as inconclusive. And the photographs were certainly not what I had hoped.

*I understand that there is also a government research program devoted to—*
There is a gentleman in the government wildlife bureau who will return phone calls regarding the Kind cat, yes. But a research program that does not make. His actual work is with their bear racial purity program.

*I'm sorry?*
The government is very concerned that the bears who have always populated this region, from west of the Carpathians through this forest and up to the peninsula in the north, are now interbreeding with a smaller bear species, the red bear, which traditionally has lived much further east, all the way to Siberia, but which because of habitat destruction has recently been crossing the Carpathians for the first time.

*It's called the red bear?*
I know, this is truly his name. Isn't it wonderful? He is often a scavenger and will live under porches or in barns or sheds, he is seen as quite a pest. And thus unworthy as a mate for the noble bear of this nation. *[Waves his hand.]* So you can see the government's priorities.

*You are not a citizen of this country, but emigrated here from—*

Yes, of course, the country I was born in no longer exists. We were amalgamated by the communists and then broken apart again by their successors and the UN, all this you know. I came to this country in the '70s.

*What inspired your emigration?*

I no longer wished to receive money from the government, which was, naturally, the only way of operating a laboratory under the communist regime.

*So you moved your research here.*

You are a very optimistic young woman. No, I moved myself. I worked for some time as an electrician illegally, and attempted to establish to the government that my education was legitimate and my scientific skills useful. I was then hired in a disease management program for dairies. I worked in this field—if you will—for eight years. A Kind cat began preying on one of the dairies on the southern border of the forest—now it is very fancy there, shops and that, what is it, paddleboating on the lake, but then it was still a very simple place, the forest surrounding it old growth. When the Kind cat came there, I was able to convince the regional government to fund my study. They are interested when extinct species return from the dead to kill off livestock.

*But others claim that this too was not truly the Kind cat, and that the official date of the cat's extirpation, 1937, should still stand.*

I am of course familiar with these arguments. But I do not know what these men believe was killing those cows, who were inarguably dead. The Kind cat has a quite distinctive track—an enlarged middle lobe on the front heel pad—and there were clear prints in blood on the flank of several of the slaughtered cows.

*Others argue that this print is easily mistaken, since a Eurasian lynx print when smeared might falsely appear to have the Kind's enlarged lobe.*

Perhaps to them, but never to me. It is not difficult to tell a blurred from a crisp impression, particularly in blood. The cow's hides were very smooth, and the evidence was unquestionable and well documented. In any case, it convinced the government to give me the lab, over the ruckus of the skeptics at the time, and the government consists largely of idiots who do not wish to spend money on anything that is of no immediate benefit to them or does not go straight into their own pockets, so the standards were sufficiently high.

*Your work is no longer funded by the government, however.*

I would not be so free with my opinion if it were. I am fortunate to have become well enough established that I must no longer be as diplomatic. This is a great luxury, particularly for a man such as myself, who grew up under a regime that denied all freedom of expression. Perhaps you cannot imagine, swaddled in the tenets of democracy as you are. *[Coughing.]*

*May I get you a glass of water?*

My coffee is directly behind you, on that shelf.

*It's cold. Would you—*

Since I am the one who placed the cup on that shelf

three hours ago, I anticipated its temperature even as I requested it. I will enjoy it regardless.

*[I hand him the cup; he drinks off the liquid.]*

*Your research is now funded by the multinational agricultural company Kreuzburg Bio.*

That is correct, and a matter of public record.

*What convinced them to fund your research into an allegedly extinct animal? It is an unusual direction for them, is it not?*

That is really a private matter. I persuaded several members of their board of the importance of the project. They sponsor hundreds of philanthropic scientific endeavors around the world, and this is certainly one of the cheapest, a pencil dot in their budget, no one even notices this old man in his woods. *[He smiles and returns the coffee cup to me, presumably to replace on the shelf, a tremor in his hand as he extends it.]*

*Why don't we use this as a jumping-off point to discuss the details of your project, then—a sense of your daily research routine, yearly cycles, if you don't mind.*

I am working to document the existence of the Kind cat, incontrovertibly. The specifics are all the specifics of a scientific study and of no interest to your magazine.

*Why not let me decide that?*

Your magazine is read by well-educated housewives and businessmen waiting for their well-educated housewives to bring them a drink. *[Chuckling.]*

*Perhaps some of those housewives have bachelor's degrees in biology, and there's our audience. [He does not laugh. He runs his hands along the lap of his trousers, one thumb still trembling.]*

*You have a number of camera stations set up in the woods. [I gesture toward the row of small TV screens.]*

Fine observation.

*[He thumps his hands against his knees, then resumes.]*

I use camera traps, with the urine of female cats in heat—not Kind cats, of course, but the urine of related species, which I have adjusted—set up in a sponge-drip system with a motion-activated camera. It is a common kind of apparatus. I also have a range of methods by which I look for physical evidence, in the form of scat, prints, and other markers of the Kind cat's movement through potential hunting territories. Its ideal territories when I began my work have now all been encroached upon by development, so I have had to continually readjust the area under study, which is both a great inconvenience to me and of course a considerable threat to the surviving Kind cat populations.

I also collect information from the inhabitants of this region, about their own sightings and sightings that have been recorded and preserved in their oral or written traditions.

*I would be interested to hear about the traditional stories of the Kind cat. Its name, for instance—I understand that it received this moniker because it preys on children?*

Yes, yes, but by this logic we could all be named for enjoying lamb or chicken fetuses, you understand. The name is unfair—unkind, even *[chuckles]*. But this is its origin. It is the largest and most lithe of the lynxes, and almost never preys on full-sized adults, but somewhat more often, though still infrequently, on smaller or weaker humans, such as children, this is very unfortunate. Usually the Kind cat must be sickly or have lost its territory to resort to this hunting behavior. In the old days there were tales that the strongest children could resist the attack and then the cats, as a mark of admiration, would teach them some of their hunting techniques. So that the best hunters and fighters in the village might be said to have been taught by the Kind cats. This was an expression used in the village I grew up in, for instance, for the strongest boys.

*I didn't realize the cat's range extended that far south, to your birthplace.*

Yes, of course, they used to be everywhere, from the North Sea nearly all the way to the Mediterranean. They are left here only because this is the largest undisturbed habitat. In my country the last century was particularly hard on them. The collectivization efforts greatly diminished their territory, and during the wars people lived in the forests, driving them out. And of course once there were people in the forests, the forests were bombed *[waves hand]*. It is funny, but even the boys who were said to be the Kind cats' (it was another name in my language, but means more or less the same), they were the first to be gone to the wars as well, because they were the strongest and most masculine and enlisted right away.

*But not you?*

No, I was a small, smart little boy, with no father.

*I'm sorry.*

He was not dead, but imprisoned. He had been a newspaper editor, but with the beginning of the dictatorship he left the city for the village of my mother's people to escape attention. There he became a teacher and had a small bookstore, but ultimately he was discovered and imprisoned for his earlier political affiliations. No doubt one of the villagers betrayed us.

*[I wait a short time.]*

*There were many rumors of the Kind cat, during the World War.*

Yes, as I said, people were living in the forests, so there were many sightings.

*Even though the cat had officially been declared extinct?*

"Official" does not mean anything. You seem to have great faith in it. But the universities and the governments were in the cities, what did they know of what happened in the big dark woods? *[Does not chuckle.]*

*The cats were rumored to feed on the war's dead. This story is told in areas across Europe.*

All cats will eat carrion, under the right circumstances.

*These were the mass graves of the Jews, to be clear.*

Yes, mostly Jews. Though many others as well. Many of the people of my village and the nearby villages were hiding in the woods at this time. The squads had begun coming through to the west of us and we had heard rumors of what happened when they reached a town. They arrived in our region after that winter, which allowed some a chance to flee, and most went to the woods. Although many died there in the winter, so it was not much of an escape. But I myself, given the choice, would certainly prefer to die in the woods.

*Do you think that this widely held belief—that they fed on the mass graves of the Jews—has permanently besmirched the reputation of the Kind cat, in the public eye?*

I do not think the public knows or cares about the cat at all. Or thinks very much at this point about the graves of the Jews. You know, it is very strange, your question, because in the old days—the days of blood libel, I'm sure you have read of these days, they did exist—it was said the Kind cat and the Jews had a particular relationship. That the Jews could train the cat to kill livestock and prey on the villagers' children. This was a very common story. When I conduct my interviews of the rural inhabitants in this region and other former habitats, no one mentions it, although they all must have heard it among the tales told by their grandparents. So these two myths of the Jews and the cat conflict, it seems, which is somewhat interesting, although common enough.

*You do not believe that the cats fed on the graves, that's a myth?*

It is possible, but we have no evidence. I believe it probably occurred, but was not widespread.

*If someone could prove it occurred, that would be evidence of the cat's existence beyond its official date of extinction.*

Of course.

*Although perhaps unfortunate, for the Kind cat's existence to be proved thus?*

Your thinking on this point is fallacious. The cats do not care or comprehend what we think of them, and if they are alive today, it is because they have been alive for tens of thousands of years, not because a scandal of some sort will prove sufficient to resuscitate them. In any case, whatever cats may have desecrated the mass graves, as you seem to think, somewhat hysterically, this event should be described, they would be long dead by now. Those living today are their descendants of, shall we say, eight generations. Great-great-great-great—and so on, you understand me—grandchildren. And you must admit that, in the animal kingdom, the kill of another predator is what we might call fair game.

*But isn't it also true that the parent company of Kreuzburg Bio, which funds your research, invented the pesticide that would later be used for mass murder in the death camps?*

That is also true.

*But this does not keep you from working with them.*

Obviously not. Is this what you are interested in?

*Is what what I'm interested in?*

This belated exposé, a few wars too late. The genocidal cats, the evil corporation *[sweeps hand briskly, one horizontal movement]*.

*No, I am interested in the cat itself.*

You have asked few questions about her. She is very beautiful. You will need to spend some time in my archives, where I have an extensive collection of photographs and artistic portrayals.

*I've reviewed many in my research, but yes, I would of course like to see yours.*

They are downstairs. We will go shortly. But what inspired your interest in her?

*The Kind cat?*

Yes.

*I'm writing a series on things that are disappearing, or have disappeared. I explained this in my letter to you.*

You went on for a long time about glaciers and, what was it, the people of certain tidal flats, but the connection is very tenuous. If you are to be a science reporter, you should know that *disappears* is rarely the correct word.

*No?*

Most things, if they are truly gone, were killed off.

*Would you mind taking me into the woods, at dusk, to the location of your last sighting?*

There would be no point. She will not come there again.

# ALICE

*I* first met Modigliani in Hibiscus Square, which he never quite owns up to. I've heard him tell the story a few times, always falsely but with such assurance I know this must be how he always tells it, or thinks of it, if he thinks of it: how we met.

Everyone who'd come to cover the hurricane, to investigate, speculate, or decry, almost all of us were living in the same situation. There were no hotels, nothing, not anywhere nearby. Several state routes and both major interstates had been washed out and on what roads remained the traffic was deadly. Any motels, campsites, or home stays in the area had gone to the displaced. There were one or two trailer parks, then, for everyone: journalists, NGO types, government employees who moved independently, carpetbaggers, volunteer coordinators, and researchers who despite their credentials seemed like the shadiest of all. They were conducting various post-catastrophic sociological studies, spoke in jargon and tried to discuss how important it was to seize opportunities for this kind of fieldwork, particularly given the wealth of post-catastrophic environments the future would offer. After all, climate change was expected to make refugees of up to a fifth of the world's population—a statistic that one of the women always inserted with a mournful delivery that I despised. We journalists more or less universally shunned the academics, relegating them to two or three trailers on the outskirts of the park, which were some of the nicest, it was realized later and with regret, but violent takeover was beyond us, we were all the type who got even warier when drinking, singing for hours, fucking, telling stories, but almost no true ones.

And so I had been living for weeks in a trailer with three roommates, only two of whom I'd met. Jeff was a photographer I knew well, and Marcos some friend of his who worked in indie radio. Marcos knew Modigliani, or knew of him. It's just somewhere to sleep, Marcos explained as he presented us with the duffel bag of a fourth roommate. He then charged the man's cell phone for him, which Jeff and I, on the floor positioned strategically near a bottle of bourbon, mocked. We told him a new roommate was fine, but he had to take the last shower, a joke we enjoyed too much at that time, our trailer had no shower and the sink was so backed up we spat toothpaste out the window, a rite that left a distinctive residue over the sill and down the outer wall to the dirt below.

At night sometimes I heard someone come in, and sometimes a T-shirt I didn't recognize hung on the makeshift clothesline. But of the man himself, nothing.

Under better circumstances I would have had more of a reaction to this situation. But in those first few days after the storm it seemed that hell had manifested in the heart of our own republic. Returning each night from a thing like that it didn't seem important to interrogate whoever might be in the next bed over. At first they said 10,000 were dead. Then it was fewer, but who was to count, corpses could be seen face-down on the street, there in a cul-de-sac, there wrapped in a tarp, and months would pass before the feds discovered those who had drowned in their homes, spray-painted a body count on each door. They found a hospital where forty-five had died in their beds or the halls, seventeen from euthanasia hastily administered. That story alone would take years to know how to tell. We all wanted in to the worst-hit districts, the big names skimmed overhead in helicopters nonstop. On the news ceaselessly people shouted from rooftops, desperate and thirsty, waving shirts and signs and surrounded by foul water. *The water is rising.* No rescue boat would waste space on us and what other ferrymen were there? For what price? One day I went out in a dinghy and water flooded my boots as I stepped over a windowsill and helped two young men out of an attic, one of them, his teeth chattering too hard to speak, slipping his hand damply into mine.

The living and the dead crowded the overpasses. The heat was unforgiving. Bridges descended like dark tongues deep into the water.

Out on the boats you couldn't tell what you might be crossing over—I rotated maps and murmured questions like a fool.

The question heard everywhere: where was the government? One by one the toilets at the stadium clogged. Day and night thousands waited in the heat on the asphalt for buses that had yet to come. On the news young men clutched garbage bags, water to their chests. Women left abandoned grocery stores with overstuffed plastic sacks. Two boys hoisted a TV over the shit in the street.

Rumors had been circulating that militias were laying siege to certain neighborhoods. In their sightlines so-called looters, anyone who might cross a bridge, anyone with dark skin in the night, so we heard. This was what brought me to Hibiscus Square that day: to interview a transitional housing coordinator whose office was on a side street off the square. She was said to know more about the vigilantes and to have had contact with some of their victims.

Xenith had arrived in the city swiftly. Most of the National Guard were still deployed abroad and according to the governor supplementary assistance was badly needed. Before that day in the square I'd seen the contractors only a few at a time, usually around food and medicine distribution centers or providing security to water treatment plants and other facilities. No one was willing to state on record what threats there may have been to these sites. Six or eight armed men in black uniforms were positioned around the square. A small rally had been planned for noon to protest socioeconomic and racial inequality in the allocation of transitional housing resources. I didn't want to get caught up, but on seeing my press pass people kept grabbing my arm, pulling me further into the amassing crowd. The crowd was much bigger than it seemed anyone had anticipated, it overflowed the once-flowering park at the square's center and extended all the way to the mouths of side streets, including the one that was my destination. Excuse me, I said again and again.

When shots were fired I heard myself shouting, Get down! Get down! and then Hold your fire! though who could have heard me, the screaming had started, I couldn't see the bloodshed from where I stood but it was as if we could smell it, the panic was instant. Stay calm! I shouted, but I was being pushed to the ground, into a deadly position, panicked feet tripping over my calves: I kept kneeling, arms around my head, and as from one side weight bore down against me, from another a hand on my arm yanked me upright, and this was Modigliani. His grip was painful. In the path through the crowd that he pulled me along, I saw one man's gun aimed our way. I threw myself toward Modigliani, shoved us both behind one of the square's enduring dogwoods. I don't know if the bullet would have hit him, and in any case we would learn that the bullets were rubber: many had been injured but no one killed. We stood pressed close to the tree for a long moment, sirens arrived, the screaming quieted and things seemed to calm. I turned to him, extended a hand and said, Thank you.

When he didn't thank me in turn I was furious.

Let me get you home, he said. I protested. But although I meant to stay and get quotes, seize this new story, instead I followed where he led, his hand still tight on my arm. I'll write in the trailer, I thought, make some calls. I was exhausted.

I had sweat through both my shirts and so had he.

We walked at least another mile in the heat. Even on the sidewalk he kept his hand on the small of my back.

Whittier Park, I said, as we got into his car.

Are you all right? he said, looking at my legs, where bruises were beginning to flower and throb in the air conditioning.

I'm fine, I said.

Someone should tell those boys they're not in Baghdad anymore, I said.

Modigliani nodded.

Are you a cop of some kind? I said.

Yes, he said, and tried to smile.

Modigliani was almost handsome back then, his oversized eyes best flattered by a few days' beard.

I don't remember our conversation. The whole time I wanted to understand whether he was thinking of himself as some kind of hero, extending the necessary chivalry by accompanying me home; or if in fact he was grateful, and even embarrassed to be grateful, having noted the rubber bullet aimed in his direction might have made contact, it seemed to me, somewhere around his neck, in which case this consideration was an attempt to acknowledge and pay back his debt to me.

When we arrived at the park, he left the car in the least muddy stretch by the road and we began the long walk trailerward, around us people sitting under makeshift awnings, working on laptops or eating McDonald's out of bags that would soon join the carpet of mud and fast-food wrappers. Others were lined up for the solar showers by the scrubby woods to the east. Modigliani and I walked in the same direction a while before it occurred to me I could let him off the hook, and I pointed at my trailer and said:

That's me right there.

I guess we're roommates, he said, and his tone failed to reveal whether this was news to him.

After a pause I said: Thought I recognized your T-shirt.

I've been meaning to pick up a new pack, he said, and we ascended the steps to the trailer. A few minutes later, clothes changed but face still pale, he headed back out. I had washed my face and was sitting on my cot watching my bruises color. See you later, he said.

I nodded and started to thank him again but cut myself off.

After he left I took a look in his bag: some shirts and pants, folded, a few nutritional bars, and a set of headphones, nothing to plug them into.

I ate one of the bars.

When Modigliani tells the story, he doesn't mention Xenith, the rubber bullets, the hundreds who tried to run. He begins with the two of us approaching the trailer from two directions, meeting at last, already roommates for weeks, at its door. In his story our surprise is mutual; whenever he tells it he slides a hand over my elbow.

# GRIGORY

On the third day after the protests reached the wall they said a child had been shot. The video arrived in my email: *you seen this yet???* You spoken to Tal today? Miriam asked from the kitchen, no need to answer, she was already dialing and I picked up the extension in my study. Tal was at his office, like always—I'm at the office, he said, what do you want? Are you all right? we said. Come stay with us, we said, till the protests are over. You always act like we're so far, but we're not far. Stop worrying, Dad, he said—and *Dad* is not what he called me as a child, but what his children call him. The protests had begun deep in the territories, then spread to the cities, right past Tal's doorstep, and now had reached the border, where tens of thousands were rioting by the wall. It was not far. According to the news the father of the dead child was not a thrower of stones. They say he had been hiding with his son behind a parked car. First of all, there is no way to know they weren't throwing stones just before they hid. I watched the video at night, wearing Tal's old headphones, so as not to disturb Miriam. They will insist that neither father nor son were throwing stones, but the video only begins with the man and the boy crouched low by the wheel of a car. We do not see the boy's face. The man wears what could be a traditional headscarf or could have been meant to protect him from tear gas, if he were among the rioters. In the video it is difficult to tell what might be happening at any moment. And if a camera's vantage point can be so unclear, think of each soldier, trying to act in the midst of this chaos, what could anyone even see? When as a young man I walked down the hallway of my university, everyone turned toward me, toward my covered head. I was smart, very good in school, but Tal, who knows nothing of this life, was born decades later and in another country, another world, Tal once told me that according to history books the quota system did not mean they let in the best, on the contrary they let in those they thought would fail, in order to decrease the quota further, based on those poor performances. He is wrong, he does not know everything. In the country of my birth there was no better technical university and I was admitted and I did not fail. The video has run to its end again and I drag the cursor back to the midpoint, the point at which it appears that the car begins to sustain fire, at least the sound of something like gunfire grows louder, the car jolts, unless it is only the camera shuddering, but the father is looking around wildly, pulling his son and himself into the wheelbase, then pointing, saying something into the ear of the boy. And then they rise, the son first and the father behind, meaning to shield him. But the bullet that strikes the boy comes from the side. What you cannot forget is that you are not seeing this, not truly, someone is filming it. Someone who is presumably somewhere safer than on this street, in a building nearby and not in the thick of the rioters throwing stones and Molotov cocktails, the soldiers besieged. Someone in some sort of window has chosen to film this man and this boy, and with a fairly steady hand, as though aware that of all the events in the territories these weeks, this one, this street, would be

the single event of significance, or at least this is what
this person, this foreign woman journalist (as she says she
is), wants to ensure. What you see on the screen is the
boy thrust sideways, then crumpling. His clothes are reddened, as are the hands of the father, who pauses there, a
few yards from the car, as though he were not in danger,
and in embracing the boy he turns his hands toward the
sky and cries out. That is when whoever is holding the
camera seems to move out from behind it, the lens falling to the side, and at this rotated view the boy although
fallen appears for a moment to be upright, then the camera jerks once more and the recording is over. The whole
thing is easily faked, everyone knows this. The gunfire
could have been real, or not. We see only the car and the
man and the boy, we have no way of knowing how near
the gunfire is—the other end of a block, or a street over,
or it could all have been simulated, either digitally or at
the scene. Furthermore even if the location were real we
do not see any soldiers, we do not see who fires the bullet
that hits the boy. How do we know this isn't just more of
the violence inborn to the territories, them shooting their
own and blaming our soldiers as always? The voice behind
the camera tells us it is soldiers who are firing. But this
is not proof. The camera's focus is so precise—the car, the
man, the boy—nothing could be identified from the scene,
no exact location. They say the boy, eight years old, died
en route to the hospital. But there would be records of
this, hospital records, Miriam will say when I argue all
this to her. She will say, surely you could know whether a
boy is dead. She will address me in the usual manner: one
hand fusses with something, the other is turned toward
the ceiling. A boy could have died, I will tell her, but they

could have chosen any boy who died yesterday of anything and said that he was this boy in the video and the soldiers shot him. Then their son could die a martyr, this is what they want. But none of this will occur, I will not show the video clip to Miriam, who as soon as it loaded and she heard the gunfire and the camerawoman's screaming, would say, Oh why do you make me watch these things? Isn't it enough, she would say, as if anyone could know what she was referring to. She goes online rarely—never, to my knowledge, and although everyone is circulating this clip and several news sites have posted it, she will not see it unless I play it for her. And a hundred kilometers away Tal is always online, as are his children, which Miriam and I have tried to discuss with him, but we are outdated, he says. All the same, he must have ways to keep the children from seeing such things as this: fake or no, a film of a boy dying. But they live in the territories, what all they must see. We're completely safe, Dad, Tal says, the town is safe, we're in a good neighborhood, the kids have been in the pool every day, there's nothing to worry about. It is true that they are in the middle of town, and the nearest border is protected with a barbed wire fence and a guard tower where snipers can be stationed or perhaps these days always are. But these days that does not always seem like enough. I drag the bar back to the starting point and load the video again. One email with which I received it came with a list of time markers at which to click pause and read descriptions of how this instant was obviously falsified. The descriptions are often more than two paragraphs each, although the video is only two minutes and forty-one seconds long. It is enough, just to know how easily it could be faked. We cannot trust anything that's called news. Which, actually, makes this country not unlike where I was born, where the news was the world's longest joke, something whose relation to the truth you could understand only by a sort of mirror imaging: once you knew what the story wished you to believe, you could determine what the opposite of that belief was, which could then be deduced to be the logical conclusion of whatever events had in fact occurred (though their details would usually remain a mystery forever). This was a skill I learned as a young man, I said aloud in the study, Miriam was asleep. A lesson Tal's children will learn too. Although the technology is now so good, I can hardly believe it. It is to be hoped that no boy died at all, that even the records could be faked. That when the camera falls to the side and shuts off, a cue is shouted, and the boy rises.

*I* was not even thinking about the veterans when I saw him. Bill LeRoy, head of Xenith, sitting alone in the window of a little trattoria. His oversized arms looked cartoonish in a suit, moving *pane* to oil to mouth. I looked at him and for a second believed the reflection of my face superimposed over his was born not of the window glass but the sheen of his head. I went in.

Mr. LeRoy, I said, lowering myself into a chair. I had unbuttoned one more blouse button on my way in.

I'm afraid I don't recall your name, he said.

I was in Hibiscus Square, I said, and at the settlement meeting where you spoke so eloquently—hearing myself I acknowledged the tragic lack of a better line. I extended a hand: Alice—

Reporter, he said, I remember. He gestured across the restaurant, and my ejection was imminent.

Would you care to comment on the murders of two of your employees, Sergei Kovarovic and Jonathan Silverman?

I'm afraid you've been misinformed, he said. These men were with the military, not with us.

After their tours, they signed with Xenith, I said, or at least you paid them, we have records of that.

His face was chubbier than you'd think, or rather more square, his eyebrows graying into invisibility.

We extend our deepest sympathies to their families

and to these brave mens' comrades, and we thank them wholeheartedly for their service to our nation. Other than that, I have no comment.

You said all that already, verbatim, I said.

And yet I must repeat myself, he said. He swiped bread through the last splatter of sauce on his plate.

Authorities are actively investigating whether all five victims may have been targeted because of their connections to Xenith. Your company will be implicated in a homicide investigation. And I don't mean in Iraq, where you can just cut and run, I mean government contracts under scrutiny, I mean murder trials, court appearances, front-page spotlight. Do you deny that your company had relationships with all five victims, not just the two officially on record?

What do you say to those who would call this company a *shadow army*?

To put it another way: to whose army would you say your employees belong?

He was walking away, I was speaking to the carafe. Several large men had arrived to block any pursuit.

I'll have lunch, I said to the waiter behind them, reaching for LeRoy's bread basket—A menu, please.

I ordered carpaccio, which disgusted me. No one in the restaurant had a thing to say. When I left, head touched by afternoon wine, there in the shade of the restaurant's awning I discovered: Modigliani. I wasn't even surprised.

I take it that didn't go well, he said.

I said: It was just lunch.

*P*enny, I said. I stood in the doorway of her room.

Now, she's never dangerous, the case manager had said when she left me at the nurse's station. But she won't talk to you, the floor nurse had added, leading me down the hall.

I understand, I said, my research does not require an interview.

To reassure her I elaborated: My methodology requires me simply to be in Mrs. Malachy's presence. Thus I'll experience a simulacrum of her husband's working environs, insofar as is possible.

Well, the nurse said, she's not easily riled, but all the same, don't try.

How old is she now, by the way? I asked.

Shouldn't you know that? the nurse replied.

Penny's hair was graying, or gray. Framed in the window were the silos I'd parked by, snow blowing so high against them that they appeared to be shrinking. In the sunset they had an orange gleam, and Penny sat with one hand on the sill, her hair fanned over the chair back as if arranged to catch the light.

Penny turned and nodded at me, as though in recognition.

I smiled, set up the folding chair, took out my notepad.

I began:

He believed in two varieties of love, one ideal and one earthly.

I struck this out, the tip of my pencil breaking, Penny still facing the window. She had gathered herself up on the chair, hand on a thin ankle, on her wrist a silver bracelet, cheap-looking and, I imagined, a gift from the nurses.

I tried again: It is unjust to claim he did not love her. He had determined that ideal love was sacred and not to be known in this world.

I wrote: Whether she knew of his theories and her place in them, we do not know.

No: How she loved him, we do not know.

In his twenties and early thirties, the period before he met Penny, Malachy's work exhibited his characteristic wit, bursts of lyricism within a minimal dramatic structure, compelling enough to gather the city's leading actors to his theater. Including Catherine Donnelly, his great love (as he called her in his daybooks of the time and even, though rarely, decades later), by this time known solely by her stage name, Sybil. According to Gideon—whose account has been, I will argue, too widely accepted—Malachy's poetry and plays had taken on "the mighty task of recreating a truly national mythos, out of primitive folktales a body of myth to sustain a nation-state." Yet could this not also be called a labor of resolute nostalgia? Children's skip-rope songs and mothers' hearth stories so ennobled? As though to tease out even the most prominent colonial families, that they might sample this morsel, this quaint native display? The dialogue was saturated with phrases in the long-suppressed native tongue, which no one would have understood—only the most dedicated young republicans might have advanced so far in their studies; or a few old aunts in the country could have nodded toothlessly. But they would have known this performance for what it was: the language not for its own sake but to goad the colonials. Sybil headed off into the villages in the west country to perfect her accent, on the same trip and not incidentally joining a tenant farmers' protest, which drew the newspapers out for one of her notorious speeches.

Much more should be said of these performances, the notices that appeared in the papers of the time, but: Penny. Penny's back to me, her vertebrae discernible through her dressing gown. Her frame slight as in the decades of photographs, her breasts still full, at this angle I saw the curve in her shoulders born of a life bearing their weight. I imagine as a girl she'd have colluded happily with her dressmaker on necklines. Penny was from a middle-class family unlikely to attend the theater, her father an upper-level clerk in one of the shipping companies. She had come to the performance on her own, arm-in-arm with her friend Winifred, who was a niece of one of the oldest republican families, its rebellious roots extending back two hundred years (though Winifred herself made no mark on history, marrying a railroad man and emigrating in the midst of the revolutionary turmoil, dying in her third childbirth). Penny. Of course I did not know if she came *arm-in-arm*. At the window Penny was humming, an orange stratum of clouds descending. When I asked about the humming, the duty nurse said: Yes, she hums. I had wanted to ask what, but clearly it was tuneless. Or not *tuneless*—tuneless was the obvious word, and I wouldn't use it, what would that even mean, *tuneless hum*? The melody proceeded by some system; it was I who could not comprehend it. Penny had been musical as girls of her class were, able to play piano a little and sing. If she had displayed any distinctive musical ability, it had never been mentioned. Perhaps this was only because Sybil's gifts had been so extraordinary—and weren't the two drawn up for comparison in every aspect, down even to their dogs? Sybil's a purebred of exceptional devotion and independence; Penny's a scrap of a thing, famed in her husband's daybooks only for keeping them in dispute with a neighbor, whose chickens the dog habitually killed. But at seventeen Penny had come to the theater, and, since she had not been familiar with theater, a naïf, and the play was of historical import, an unequivocal achievement, would she not have smiled? "Her smile is one of the great constancies of my life," her husband wrote once in his daybook—no, in a letter to his editor. But was that, truly, praise?

I had yet to see Penny smile; I would ask the nurses.

Malachy watched every performance from a stool at the end of the front row. And one night, watching Sybil in her magnificence as the queen of the hill country, might he not have wondered: why this nostalgia? For what? A past he had spun out of spider web, fairy wing, the pagan legends anyone could unearth from the saints' tales? Fables of snakes and sylphs, generations of lost infants? If a nation were to rise again, it must have not only a past, not merely a past, but a future. And so I put aside childish things, he might have said—though not in a day, over the course of several years, after the first failed revolt and after he stopped writing for the theater and began instead an elegy: an elegy for a future republic he did not wish to lose. Penny was with him by then, wife and companion. Penny, whom apocrypha would have it on one occasion received a handgun from fleeing republicans in the streets and slipped it under the fish in her shopping basket, nodding at the uniformed thugs of the empire on the corner as she passed. Malachy dedicated his next collection of poems to her, though the civil war delayed publication, and by the time the book was released, to international if not domestic acclaim, it was commonly known that Penny was going mad.

Mad—but no one now would use this word, I must find another, clinical perhaps, more appropriate, what would the poet say, what did he? Trances, he said. The most delightful fits, he was said to joke when drinking with friends or hangers-on. According to all accounts, Penny had been badly treated at the home before this one, restrained in bed day and night. Until the patron who now funded the theater the poet had sixty years ago made famous had learned of Penny's situation through a feminist artist— she'd created out of thousands of papier-mâchéd pages of Malachy's work an oversized straightjacket, poised wretchedly in a gallery corner and titled *Penny*—and had sought out medical advice and that of the estate to remedy it. Which had resulted in Penny's transfer to her current residence. Penny had not been in her own country for decades: after the poet's death, when her family had first institutionalized her, they had sent her overseas on the recommendation of an American pharmacist cousin. Her father's decision—though since he succumbed to dementia not long after, some suspect that he comprehended little of the situation. But neither her siblings nor anyone else fought for her return. Perhaps there were bureaucratic obstacles; we might grant them this.

By my third visit, whenever I entered her room, even when I was only returning from the toilet, Penny would rise to shake my hand. She would not look at me; she looked, I believe, at the pen in my left breast pocket.

By my fourth visit, she no longer sat in the chair by the window, but on the bed, and gestured toward the nightstand to offer it. I had tired of longhand and now brought my typewriter with me, having confirmed by brief experiment that the noise did not disturb her. At first I used a traveling table I rigged myself, and poorly, so that it collapsed about once an hour—one time so violently that I had to hug the typewriter to my chest, a posture that left me covered with ink, and when my tie then caught on the keys, despite myself I swore. This was the only time I heard Penny laugh.

Mad? Penny's right eye was damaged, blood vessels a forbidding golden branching toward the iris. Her eyes— which to my knowledge the poet had never described— were hazel: a ring of brown, ring of green. If you looked her in the eye, she tipped her head sideways.

Frequently she would flick her right hand up at the waist then sweep it over her head, a girl's imitation of a dancer. Could she be remembering Sybil? Mocking her, after all these years? Penny was twelve years younger than Sybil, but Sybil had died young, in her fifties, a swift-acting cancer. She had lived to see her legitimate son serve in the parliament of her new nation and her illegitimate son become a musician of great early success and strong communist leanings, in the years since her death known best for the latter.

Sybil? I said.

Penny didn't respond. Though I could not interpret her constant small movements. Left hand tapping her thigh, feet shuffling, often with startling speed for a woman her age. Right hand twisting her hair into a tight ringlet, forefinger caught in its center.

I'm sorry, I said.

I extended a hand, but she turned back to the window.

By my fifth visit it was almost spring, snow receding, first from the depressions that were in fair weather paths between the asylum buildings, now rivulets. In dirtying heaps against the walls snow endured. I wore galoshes to walk from the car, which the head nurse smiled at condescendingly.

I sat beside Penny at the window. There was no birdsong yet, only wind.

It is said that her madness was inspiration.

I typed, then paused.

Her madness was madness.

Mad as mad.

A hornet, a March hare, a wet hen, hell.

And *this* was my argument, what would distinguish me. In his 1958 study, Abernathy claimed to have definitively traced lines of the poems of that period to their origins in journals the poet kept of his wife's Trances (his capitalization; or TRANCES). Abernathy's study, originally a monograph discussing solely the long poem "Carousel as Seen by a Cyclist in Motion," was extended into book length upon further access to the archives, and has been treated as foundational to all subsequent discussion. The tragedy of Penny's madness redeemed by its inestimable contribution to literature.

But—not merely literature. For the poet's progress was the progress of the nation: from the idealistic fervor of his early theatrical work, to the elegiac rigor of his middle period, the stately tumult of his posthumous collection. His maturity the poetic equivalent of beating sword into plowshare: the man's work had begun, and the man was visionary. The nation could now be seen and heard; within this lifetime the nation would come into being. If words could conjure it, and they would. A few short years after Penny's first night at the theater, street signs were nailed up bearing the old names, in the old tongue; scholars turned from preservation, huddled over transcribed songs and illumined manuscripts, and wrote children's textbooks, used first in the west then in the capital. The republicans formed committees, drafting constitutions and labor agreements, to ready the economy for independence. When the colonial forces turned their guns on a crowd at a football match, the next day's streets were not cowed into silence, but loud even with mothers and children in protest, the threats of strike made good on nationwide, and before the end of the week twelve of the empire's top men in the city had been assassinated, by bomb, by gun, in one case a knife wielded by his own tailor.

The archives of the colonial parliamentary committee meetings attest: they knew they were staring down the barrel. The days of the order they'd always known were ending. They thought no longer of how they might prevail but what might be borne away with them in their routing. *Not least our dignity, not least our lives*—as the famous line would have it, exclaimed behind closed doors by the prime-minister-to-be.

Who could not see that the time had come?

Penny?

And isn't this the question upon which everything relies? Was she visionary—how clearly she could see the new nation, her mind gone in the light of the city on the hill—or was she blind? Soothsayer, or mere babbler? Her words flotsam or the surf's very pounding, through which the poet could hear the moon?

Others tell us of Penny's speech, name it a torrent, inconceivable chaos. But the poet claimed to transcribe all she would say in her spells. What he called the truth of the Trance, or Truth. She talked, her sister said in an interview, my God, did she talk; but her sister rarely visited, having married determinedly into the bourgeoisie and since then having been mocked by Malachy every time she opened her mouth. Other scholars have attempted to locate the couple's servants from the time, but these interviews have yielded no further insight into the manifestation of Penny's illness, the substance, as it were, of her insanity, material of the vital discourse. The poet hailed her speech as the mother-tongue. "It is in these Trances," he wrote, "that she attains the higher state of being to which we may only aspire."

But is this statement not perfectly bland?

Is it not the least persuasive line in the body of his writing?

One cannot ignore—though others have minimized—the terrible incident. The theater was closed and the civil war in its sickening final months. The best of that generation of revolutionaries were dead, put to death by the empire or, the last, the greatest, the leader the nation deserved: ambushed in the hills and shot between shed and barn by his own countrymen. The hero fallen, and what would become of the state whose dream he had bled? In these months, the nation destroying itself from within, no books forthcoming and creditors clamoring, the poet had implored Penny not to go to her family for money—the sister whom he despised, the traitorous father who would work for the shipping masters until the day they fled with their wives and children—but to take on work, light sewing or laundry, to help pay the bills. Yet her illness must already have been progressing; he had been noting his concerns in his daybook for months, and his sister Margaret's letters to him spoke of little else. "There is a strange cast to Penny," the sculptor and anarchist known as Dragoman, who was living in exile and spent much of those years among the poet's circle, had written. "She rarely looks at anyone or thing, but is to be found mothlike drawn to the window, and answers questions only after they are repeated three or four times, or her husband goes to her and asks them again in his own voice. Malachy does not seem distressed, but arranges himself at the windowsill beside her, hardly interrupting his own tirades, but holding her hand between his own; inevitably her gaze floats again to the window, even in the dark. At night one awakes to a murmur rising through the floor, through the bowels of the house, that I believe is her speech." (This a passage I had read in no other study; Dragoman kept his journals in a devilish blend of English and his native Cyrillic-based dialect, which has only recently been authoritatively translated.) Some have suggested, without condemnation, that the poet did not send Penny to her family for money because he feared they might notice her illness and involve themselves; naturally he distrusted them. Fortunately, their financial crisis was averted: an

American paper requested an occasional poem from him upon the ambush of the rebel hero that was the nadir of the civil war. This led to other commissions, and soon a collection was accepted by the Boston house Hayworth & Brent.

It is not that my argument is original: in his three-volume biography Gideon too suspects that the poet's records of Penny's speech are fabrications; thus she was more puppet than muse. Yet to him this suspicion is of little consequence. (We may almost envy Gideon his chauvinism: he is the only biographer who does not dedicate more pages to Sybil than Penny, but dispenses efficiently with both.)

But I—I who pass these hours with Penny—shall prove this suspicion to be sea change, a thread that when pulled unweaves the tapestry. Malachy's diaries of her Trances, those Abernathy claims as the wellspring of his greatest poems—I shall establish each word in them is Malachy's, there is no trace of Penny. Their spiraling metaphors, distinct syntax, insistent iambs: his and his alone. That he claimed otherwise is evidence merely of a last myth he would offer and cannot be cited as proof. She spoke; but if we have only his testimony of what she said, we have nothing.

Which brings me here and makes a fool of me. Thinking it might suffice, to bring a pen like his, a typewriter of the same model, draw near to her and wait. When I was warned that she has not uttered a word in years. With no particular concern the nurses affirm this.

Penny—if her speech was no prophecy, what was it? How may we know the river of her mind, by whose banks a man composed? A land and a people extending in every direction and breaking into dawn. For if the words were his, hers are lost, a dream of wind or stone. The man who claimed to be vessel of revelation offered only himself, robed in lore, a costume to deceive the ages.

What Penny thought of him, poised beside her, notebook in hand, we do not know. If he ever endeavored to listen.


The civil war ends. The poet's politics—now funded in their expression by his American publisher, whose enthusiastic young editor (later the most eminent in the Boston literary scene) wrote him weekly whether there was business or not—began to harden. He moved toward the center-left position for which he would be criticized by the upcoming generation of radicals and writers, those singing the praises—for a time, before the bombings intensified—of the burgeoning guerrilla movement then beginning its first series of strikes in the north. The poet's youthful soft spot for anarchism would become, I will establish, merely aesthetic, of no political value, sentimental as his love for a madwoman.

Penny was barefoot in the gardens, Penny was under the stairs, her voice a fretful echo in the floorboards. If you hadn't seen her in hours, you could whistle for the dog, and he would lead you to her. Penny sat outside the army barracks in the village, with a basket of sewing—this the most famous story, like the others unproved. Sybil could come by the house and Penny would not know her to despise her; they could walk together barefoot, the poet watching from his study window.

Write again for the theater, Sybil would argue with him.

I will not write if you will not act, he replied, though this was not the reason.

I no longer read M's poems, Sybil wrote in her diary: when the urge comes over me, just as I've gotten into bed, to pick up the volumes of his I still keep treasured, instead I turn to the most recent treatises of the Agrarian Socialist Movement, and I am soothed, and I sleep.

How pretty your poems are, Sybil said to him, at dinner one night, their last great public spat, not long after the birth of her second son. What a pretty commonwealth we must have. You must—and with this in his daybook he claims she seized his tie and flicked it against his chin— have all your coats laundered regularly, to be sure the blood of our martyrs hasn't spattered upon you, you do like to stand so close and watch.

For some time I had thought the poet invented this incident, so vividly did he recount it. But I have now discovered a letter, from a journalist present that night, and perhaps Sybil's lover, that confirms it in every detail.


By my sixth visit, Penny will fall asleep in my presence, waking only when I stop typing. She sleeps in her chair, spittle shining on the shoulder of her dressing gown. The bulbs are coming up, the first few, which will have to suffer at least one more frost.

On my seventh and eighth visits, I bring the others' biographies with me, the whole stack. I read aloud to Penny every chapter about her. I think her humming may grow louder, or more monotonous. I read the chapters about Malachy's childhood, since perhaps there are things she may never have known. I read a few of the poems from his last collection, published posthumously: she was reportedly too sick to have read them.

By my ninth visit, when I open a book, Penny lies down, her head at the foot of the bed, near me. I read her the newspaper: in the north of her country a car bomb has been detonated, downtown in a suburb, not by the jail or courthouse, but by the shops, the bus stop. Fourteen policemen have been assassinated in the last year, latest count. Most of the leaders of the new resistance, the most ardent young men, are now in prison, where it's said they wake and sleep covered in their own feces, and sculpt the food they are given into rot on the walls. Their hair grows long and is forcibly cut from them; they are beaten and hosed clean of the excrement in which they have clothed themselves, demanding political recognition, the full panoply of rights. The old tongue has faded again, I tell her, is used only in signs for tourists. I offer her a handful of postcards of the west country beaches, where she and the poet traveled in their youth, when she still had her health and the revolutionaries still had ties to tenant farmers and the collectivization efforts underway in those days. Penny has fallen asleep. I leave the postcards on the windowsill. What we lack now is a poet, I say upon closing the newspaper, and imagine her reply.

*T*he investigation was going nowhere. If Modigliani thought otherwise, he didn't let on. There were no arrests, no signs of progress, and the official interviews had gone into reruns. Leads the cops reassured us of in statements seemed to end there. As far as I could tell it was just Modigliani hitting the pavement.

What I'm saying is, there was no story. A fact it was hard to believe but each day confirmed. I had profiles of the victims, tons of background. In my notes I used their first names, hoping to call them up, make them feel known: Kareem, Frances, Jonathan, Sergei, Diana. I'd looked into the PTSD study. Compared it, in methodology and results, as far as I could assess, with studies around the state and country. Nothing of note. I started working on VA hospital stats, but that path was well-trod. I went back to Xenith.

Xenith landed in Baghdad in the heady days just after the invasion, didn't miss a beat and in fact had beaten me there. I'd sat alone in an airport bar watching the shock and awe, firestorm in the night of an ancient city. It seemed that almost as soon as we freelancers had sorted our visas, stepped off the plane, charged our laptops, Baghdad had fallen. So there we were: birth pangs of an occupation. Coalescing around us what would be known forever after as the *heavily fortified Green Zone.*

I was there, I thought I was good to go. I'd found an interpreter but within a day lost him to the death of his mother. I could have tagged along here or there, made it work, but I caught some bug and spent day after day in my room sweating, thick-headed.

From my window I saw a war. A Marine unit doing sweeps, the same one always, I suspected, by my glimpses of a boy's orange hair. Humvees and occasional tanks forced themselves down the street, fat cats squeezing through a pet door, I thought, feverish and tired of metaphors. I listened: sirens, traffic, distant explosions, it could have been a TV set to static. In the room next to mine a man shouted in an unknown language.

Once a day I forced myself out of the hotel and to a local teahouse, not the one where I was most welcome. I interviewed the regulars, but got little, no one wanted to talk to a flushed soft-eyed American, damp with some disease out of the heartland. I filled a notebook with sketched maps, brief interviews, impressions of the smells and prayer song, the migration of bursts of gunfire across the horizon. I photocopied a fourteen-year-old's diary, loaned to me by its author. I think I believed that one day all this would signify something. Testify to something in the boundless history of war.

Walking too slowly back to my hotel one afternoon I ran into none other than my ginger Marine, hair just visible beneath his helmet. I nearly greeted him before remembering he wouldn't know me. But he must have seen my expression on the verge of warmth, and from that day whenever he saw me he stopped me to chat. I couldn't seem to avoid him.

The second time we met he pulled a handful of vitamin C packets out of a pocket and offered them, saying: I gotta say, you look like shit.

Thanks, I said, and wiped at the snot dried on my face.

More where that came from, he said: Embed with us and reap the rewards.

He looked pleased with himself. He looked not a day over twelve.

Goes against almost everything I believe in, I said.

I'm just talking good old-fashioned military-friendly journalism, he said. What's not to love?

I'll think about it, I said.

Don't cry now, he said.

My eyes didn't stop watering the whole time I was in that country. In my room I drank fizzing glasses of vitamin C, though I suspected it was far too late. Every day my interpreter called to say he'd be back tomorrow and for the first ten days I believed him. The truth was I didn't care, or I cared too much. I stayed in bed. You all right? came the knocks at the door and a baby laughed on speakerphone through the wall. I thought, maybe this was the body's natural response, or should be. To shut down, not go on with business as usual, if that's what you could call foreign correspondence. I believed—no, something less than believed—that in my passivity I might claim a perspective no one else could, if I could exist in time so slowly, moment by moment as around me a nation fell to its knees, if I watched my ceiling and heard the long coda of an invasion, I would know something. Something else? Something more true? Looking back I can't defend myself, can't say what *more true* might mean, though at the time I wrote the phrase surprisingly often. I'd begin with the men, long dead, who had sat around a map and drawn the borders of what we know as Iraq. I would lead in with the history of colonialism, the fall of the US's groomed leaders, the rise of the nationalists and theocrats. The gas attacks in the north we'd closed our eyes to, the weapons we'd sold. I would depict not just the scene before me but the motion of time within it, the forces of history that had pushed this nation to this wall, oil wells lit in the fields and not a flower thrown at our feet.

But I was silent, I was a woman, sick in a room. No country confessed its secrets to her. A people, a history, a language, a god, not one truth, though she waited attentive on street corners, notebook open for days. Every word I wrote anyone could have written. I filed some stories I don't care to remember. Around me my colleagues and rivals assembled and I was slow to follow, looking off to the side, to the sky, to the ditches, the hands of children, begging or selling or waving a flag. Looking anywhere but at the page that was supposed to be mine. I walked the streets in a haze and if I turned toward anyone, I knew what they saw: a woman who did not share their fate.

You're sick, the others said, when I tried to explain. Sweetly they left brandy at my door.

Alice! one day a voice cried behind me. I was leaning on a blast wall outside a half-empty market, watching the stalls get set up, rugs unroll. This was before the market bombings started.

How do you know my name? I asked Ginger, who was now beside me, pleased as any puppy.

He winked.

How's the unembedded life? he said.

I love the taste of freedom, I said.

Come with me, he said. I have some real shit to show you.

Reader, what should I have said?

*I* am writing to you regarding Ibrahim. I have waited to write, too long. I would call but over the phone my accent is strong, I am told.

I am a photographer. I did not work with Ibrahim officially but for a French news service. I was partnered with a reporter, and he and I traveled with Ibrahim often, four or five of us all together, because we got along and because there are many official tours in this war, often you end up on helicopters or buses full of journalists. We are marched around in little groups and everyone we manage to speak to is anxious that we report they are winning— we've learned that if it is said you have yielded an advantage, you will pay a price. Ibrahim has perhaps told you this. I do not mean to presume.

Ibrahim said that he did not like to tell you the worst stories until at least a month later because then they would be only the past. A month is long enough, he explained. A new moon. He believed that even in the city people notice the moon more than they know. I imagine he has shared this theory with you.

Something beautiful that Ibrahim and I once saw: in the river that divides these two countries, a river which is in fact the juncture of two great rivers, an oil tanker had been trapped for three weeks. The captain was frightened by the attacks on civilian vessels and would not move the tanker unless it was guaranteed an escort all the way to the gulf. By now there was fighting all around it, tank guns trained on it from the eastern banks, and even the gulf had been mined. This is not the point. For several days the tanker had kept its lights on through the night. I could not say why. But these ships are enormous, and when one is lit up like that, lit on every level and in every aperture, floodlights illuminating each bare deck, it is so bright, so bright that it can hurt to see. You see this offense of light, near enough to the mouth of the river that the tide touches it twice a day, and you know then what a miracle light is. Power. In the belly of this tanker. But this is not what I called beautiful. Imagine a night like this, a yellow beast in the river. The moon is almost full, and its yellowing face looks to you like not a reflection but a mockery of the scene below, the mammoth ship pinned and unblinking. Tonight Ibrahim and I are on the western side, in a dock area that has been abandoned since the beginning of the war. The tanker is Canadian and Ibrahim is enjoying this, acting out little dialogues that include everything we know about Canada, which is little. The only one who isn't laughing is Bertrand, the reporter I am working with, and he rarely laughs at anything, except the sight of very young whores, though not out of cruelty. But picture the moon. It is strange to think of. Bertrand says something about the moon, pointing at its reflection on the water. The reflection of the moon can at this moment be distinguished from the tanker's relentless reflection—on the surface of the river a sphere, deformed and lovely. The light around the tanker looks like a fluorescence of creatures suckling at its hull.

But then a fleet of shadows crosses, disturbing the moonlight, like a rush of dark fish through the yellow glow. Ibrahim is the one who understands. Run, he says, shells, and as he says this they explode, not far behind us, and terribly, terribly loud. Ibrahim is pulling me and Bertrand is running ahead. The Australian, Daniel, is slow—he had twisted an ankle jumping down from one of the wretched helicopter tours. But Ibrahim grabs him by the wrist. Someone's sweat smells to me like sweetgrass left out to hay, though perhaps this odor comes somehow from the shelling.

We run northward along the bank, to an abandoned shipyard. We all survive, and the explosions were not that close to us, although the ringing in the ears takes some time to subside. Above us the sky the shells traverse does not reveal them: death so quick you see only its shadow.

The next morning I thought of you, in a way: I thought that a few days before the next full moon, Ibrahim may tell Sarah this story.

No one has told you how Ibrahim died. I was the only one there, the soldiers and I. I did not tell his editor this story, although you may, if you wish. I do not mean I am telling you what to do. I considered contacting Ibrahim's editors, but he spoke so often of you. It was not that he talked of your and his past, rather plans, or qualities he ascribed to you—he would interrupt himself, shaking his head, and say, if Sarah could hear me, she'd be shaking her head. I do not claim I knew him well.

The essential thing to understand is that one country has five times the population of the other. Five times. This means five times the army. And this means that the Deputy (this is all his name means, in translation, this is important to remember)—who calls the opposition a wave of insects he is prepared to exterminate—has to kill large numbers of troops while losing next to none. This is the only strategy by which he may win the war he began. Along the easternmost river, one of the two I have mentioned, which serves as the border between the two nations and thus as a perpetual front, there are ancient marshlands. Both sides have advanced through them; most recently troops came in great force from the east, which was a considerable territorial acquisition; they were only a few dozen kilometers from the highway that leads to the capital. There are people who live in the marshlands. Tribes is what they are usually called, marsh people. I grew up among what you might call hill people (I was sent away for school, as you can tell, I was lucky; it was during the civil war and not a good time to be a young man at home). My people are hill people, goat people, even though my family is rich: they are surrounded by goat and sheep and hill people, and so that's what they are as well. The marsh people are marsh people, is what I mean.

When they saw the enemy coming through the marshland, the Deputy's general bombed huge stretches of the marshes, lit everything that could be lit. There are animals there that live nowhere else in the world, several species of which are now gone. The bombs lit the reeds and reed houses, plants of all kinds, the rice fields. Then the Deputy's soldiers ran cables through—through the marshes themselves, and this is kilometers. They electrified the water and everything in it: enemy soldiers, their own people, the marsh tribes, fish, water buffalo, gazelles. A day after this Ibrahim and I arrived.

I believe we were the only ones allowed into this place. Ibrahim had very good contacts in the army, and he requested that I come with him, although as it turned out I was forbidden to take pictures. They confiscated my camera and it was only upon Ibrahim's death that they returned it.

I will not describe the place to you. We walked along a sort of dike and nothing could be worse than the stench. To our right the marshes extended and everywhere bodies floated in clusters. The water was dark with ash. As the bodies moved you could start to see that some had been slit open. I have told this story in the wrong order. We had been walking to this place for some time, from the village where the main defensive forces were stationed. We knew nothing yet of what had happened in the marshlands, except that the Deputy's general had called it a victory. The soldiers we followed wouldn't talk much, but led us to one embankment, where we stood a long time not speaking, waiting for some higher-ranking military liaison to arrive, to tell us what I don't know. Ibrahim needed to relieve himself. He walked over to one side, a ditch in the network of causeways. Then he began to scream. I have heard screaming like this before and I thought it must somehow be coming from the dead, I did not at first understand. The water was still electrified. I learned this later. In fact, although we could not see it, one of the generators was in a hut not far from us. We had no way to imagine this. The soldiers who were escorting us yelled at Ibrahim, running toward him. I reached him before they did, but the electricity had already stopped his heart. You do not want to be a piss martyr, the soldiers were calling as they ran. Piss martyr was the phrase they were using. I do not know if this was because there had been other piss martyrs or if they had only thought of this, in their time there, as a sort of joke with each other. I tried to resuscitate Ibrahim, but I am not trained, and there was no one else to summon, not in time. Probably they told you he died in an accident at the front. Do not think less of him for pissing into the marshes of the dead. I saw the ditch below him and there was no one.

I neatened him before they sent his body back.

One soldier laughed. I tell you this so that you will not wonder if anyone laughed. It is a reaction. And the soldiers there, their job was to patrol the banks of these lagoons of corpses.

I believe Ibrahim would shrug at the name, piss martyr. He would laugh. You know him better. Perhaps I am wrong. I slapped the soldier who laughed on the face, though I am sorry for this now.

Outside the VA hospital I ran into Modigliani. The crime scene had resumed its somber bustle and I was embarrassed to be there. As if Modigliani had found me wrist-deep in a jar labeled *clues*. I couldn't confront him with the failure of his investigation without claiming that failure as my own.

It could be true, what I've been suspecting, that I've lost my edge. The first installments of the hurricane stories had made a big splash, but then what—? No arrest, no resolution. On an American street in an American city someone had executed a man and a woman: a social worker and addict—former teacher—barrel of the gun right to the back of each head, a lynching too familiar and yet to this day, no thanks to me and Modigliani, too vague. What had happened that night? What could these deaths mean? Was the shooter some white-power night rider, or among the uniformed Xenith forces, trained and paid to proliferate through that city's bad dream? Or were those identities, for at least a night, indistinct? The story should end, should have ended, with a call-to-arms, a finale of sheer moral force: the unanswered questions, unavenged crimes, proclaimed again and searingly, so that someone, some public-interest lawyer, some professor with a grant, free from deadlines, from political badgering and law enforcement quotas, someone could have demanded justice. Instead Modigliani had been reassigned and I, I had trailed off. What was I to do, I asked the editors who no longer call me, run an investigation from the pages of a magazine? Witness, judge, and jury, in one byline? Once again the dead had picked the wrong champion. And once again here I was, at something like the beck and call of Modigliani.

When he saw me by the hospital door, he shook his head. Since in my experience Modigliani has never made a joke, it's hard to know what he might mean when he tries.

Got ten minutes? he said.

I wanted to say no, but I had all the time in the world.

Any progress with Xenith? he said as we walked.

I'm not sure what you were expecting, I said.

We entered the cafeteria. He picked out an egg-salad sandwich. I let him buy me a juice and we sat in the corner everyone else avoided, where the bulbs flickered spastically.

About Xenith, I said, I'm not going to do your grunt work in exchange for shit information and—I flicked the bottle—cranberry juice cocktail.

That's not what's happening here, he said. This case could be their Achilles' heel and I thought you'd be interested. This is as good an opportunity as you're likely to get.

There's a vote of confidence, I said.

Modigliani unstuck plastic wrap from the golden squish of his sandwich. You were in Baghdad with them, he said.

Yes, I said.

I knew where he was going: The three journalists Xenith had killed. I'd been thinking about it the whole time; I'd been thinking about it for years. The journalists were unarmed and everyone knew the Xenith guys were drunk, blasting through in one of their Humvees, opening fire on any group of men gathered on a corner. But the men had just been setting up a camera, to interview this local sculptor, of all people, who was initiating a series of civic art projects. After the shootings one of Xenith's top guys goes in and soon enough no one can be tried in any country. For all we knew the men—murderers—had been redeployed. I'd researched our five victims wondering if I might uncover this kind of past. Not yet.

Modigliani said: You didn't stay long in Baghdad. You were gone before the incident with the journalists, you didn't even cover it. Why was that?

He looked worse than I did, his cheeks hollowing in the unsteady light.

I was kidnapped, I said.

He didn't reply and it occurred to me he might think I was joking.

I said: I'd started going around with this Marine unit sometimes, and one day we went out to a rough part of the city, where there was a big standoff, a bunch of Marines, a peanut cleric and his ragtag militia, and these Polish forces there as a part of the coalition. By the time I got there shots had been fired. A Polish guy had been hit in the leg and one Iraqi had been shot in the stomach. He was bleeding and bleeding and beside him, two goats were dead. Sounds like the set-up for a joke. It was a very tense scene, everybody was shouting. I got there and was angling around to try to get a sense of things, heading just a little deeper into the neighborhood, when—hood, van, bam.

Christ, said Modigliani.

I'm sure they were looking to make some money, but for whatever reason—I couldn't see anything, but they sounded like kids—after three days they just dumped me. Blindfolded, hands tied, in some lot by an old brick factory, way out in one of the old Sunni neighborhoods. Or so I was told. By then I was really out of it, beyond thirsty, I spent about a day, I think, lying there, trying to cough up dust without any spit. You think that, given enough time and motivation, you could just get yourself out of whatever restraints. But you can't.

But someone found you?

Yes, I said. I said: the first guy who found me raped me. I couldn't see him, I don't know who he was. I thought that he spoke to me in English. I've never been sure if that was real or I dreamed it. The language, I mean. Later some Iraqi police found me and brought me to a hospital.

I'm sorry, Modigliani said.

I nodded and finished my juice.

You didn't have to tell me, he said.

You didn't have to ask, I said.

Only I smiled.

*I* slept in another town, far from the strawberry fields, so as not to hear the sobbing. Despite this the sobbing was all my mind in its nightly sifting of memories would settle upon; no matter the night sounds of insects and dogs it was all I heard. My dreams could have been called nightmares were they not made up of memories; it was as though I lived each day twice, once by day, once by night. And the music by which the scene recreated itself behind the curtains, each twilight to sweep open again, was the sound of sobbing.

In the town where I slept a few people had started to sicken, though this was to have been a safe zone, this is what we had been told. All the government, medical, and clean-up teams were here, reassuring and talking hope. But every day residents left, abandoning their homes, diminishing the competition in the canned food aisle. Yet the streets didn't empty, they filled: all those who answer the call of disaster had come, military contractors were stationed on every corner, to perform or prevent what I preferred not to imagine.

In the town to the west—which the media named *ground zero*, a phrase I would never use—the children sobbed, they could not be quieted. They cried in their hunger and in crying they grew dehydrated and only sicker. The children cried as we tried to speak with them or take their pictures, and then, once they were hospitalized, simply to sit beside them. Their limbs are like popsicle sticks, one news-caster ventured, later to be berated: poor taste to compare starving children to a summer day's treat. Their limbs are like sticks, some wrote. Like twigs, I almost wrote. But their size was mesmerizing: a body assembled so insub-stantially, denied any excess and thus any future, each bone's form visible, skeleton in friable miniature. The children were dying at the rate of four or five a week. New mothers who had tried to breastfeed had been in most cas-es lost soon after their infants.

Those who worked in the strawberry fields had been struck first, and this, it was suggested, caused the delay in raising the alert; the first cases had occurred among migrant workers in intervals along the route southward, and the first hospitalizations (at least the first now ac-knowledged) were south of the border. In this country those stricken were slow to seek care: uninsured, un-documented, and thus willing to endure some weeks of diarrhea. Teachers in the town's school had for months noted among themselves that those of the children who had been fat were now thin and those who had been thin were now thinner. When parents came for pick-up or conferences, they too—it was common gossip, what diets were making the rounds in the trailer parks down by the fields?—seemed on average to have shrunk, skin of the mothers' arms flapping loosely. What were the teachers to have done? The only question to ask, which more than a few did—even employing the full condescending appara-tus of interpreters and social workers—was: Are the chil-dren getting enough to eat?

Now the town was divided up into encampments in-habited by medical staff, assorted cleanup crews, security details, journalists, all of us distinguishable by our biohazard suits, huge white things with plastic-windowed faces. Distinguishable, I mean, from the town's inhabitants; not at all from one another. To recognize anyone suited you had to get quite close and face them squarely; at any angle the light off the plastic window would obscure their features or dazzle the eyes so that one couldn't make out a face. The contractors we knew by their weapons. The farm workers and townspeople had worn the suits as well for a few weeks, after the arrival of the medical teams, until the first round of testing had concluded. The tests determined that most of them had already absorbed well beyond lethally high levels of the toxin, and further exposure was unlikely to worsen the course of the illness. (And if it did—though I heard no one say this—couldn't that be for the best? To go swiftly?) Those who could still in theory be treated had been evacuated to a medical facility outside town. The hopelessness of their own condition was not conveyed to these last residents so directly, but it became understood, and soon enough the afflicted walked down the street or lay in hospital cots unsuited, the attenuated shapes of their bodies in absurd contrast to the monotone troupe the rest of us comprised, their tanned skin warm beside our own white material, although it would be fairer to, it was fairer to, describe their skin as ashen.

As the weeks passed, the local dogs grew louder and ever present, howling with hunger as their caretakers died or abandoned them. Together, leaner, nearly wild, they formed packs that fought and bayed in the streets. They massed too near the medical centers and makeshift cafeterias and were audible in the background of any gathering. We walked the streets in twos or threes for security, and even I took to carrying a stick to push them from me. Soon vans were sent for them and then they too were scarce.

The official count of the town's dead was 121, 106 of them since I had arrived two weeks ago. I didn't know how long I would stay. In my room in the town to the east—a house vacated by its owners and given over to vultures like me—I had for something like comfort stacked up and organized my cans. Corn, peas, peas and carrots, pearled onions, stuffed grape leaves, beef chili, turkey chili, baked beans and bacon, fruit cocktail, mandarin oranges, artichoke hearts, one great tower of Boston brown breads. Eight pallets of water bottles, an array of hand sanitizer. Another box of victuals was on its way from my university to the local UPS depot (even the most optimistic now conceded that anything left on a porch or stoop would be stolen). I'm not sure whom they had send it—a department secretary, I suppose, or a grad student, perhaps honored to have some role in this historic tragedy, to curate the best selection of nonperishables, box and ship them to me seven hundred miles away.

I've retired from field work, I had told the institute when they called me in, after the first reports of the situation had broken. I should have saved my breath. The curse of having written a book like mine—*essential, magisterial*, as the blurbs have it—on undocumented labor was that you could never again, even after twenty-five years, beg apathy, remain uninvolved. It's been too long and this is something else entirely, I said, but then started packing, and when I think back to those early days, my years of interviews, my time in the demonstrations, my own pathetic hunger strike (six days and I collapsed into unconsciousness, woke in shame on a feeding tube), it is as though it happened not to me, but to a lover, a beautiful young woman whose idealism was never quite naïve enough to condemn, and whom I would love to see again, to converse with or to fuck, but whom I do not know as myself. I am old now. I am not too old. Aging has been nothing like I expected, since I expected nothing that I care to recall.

And so I returned to the beat, a sixty-two-year-old woman, surrounded by so-called colleagues: journalists vibrant in youth or rugged in middle age, unwashed rough types and orange-faced idiots ready for any camera. Stupidly I'd brought nice button-downs and two blazers, not anticipating the biohazard suits. Once or twice I tried to go to a bar with the others, a forty-five-minute drive to where anything was still open, but I couldn't sit in peace there, both TVs turned to the news, and instead I took to night walks or sitting and not writing alone in my room.

I imagine that like me the others spent some minutes each day considering their shit, its quality and what it might portend.

Teams of scientists addressed us, roomfuls at a time, folding chairs set up in this church or that YMCA for briefings. The scientists and their spokespeople gave their presentations in a sort of simultaneous translation, once in proper science then once in layman's terms, enough scientific vocabulary overlaid to suggest authenticity. In the presence of sun and rain of sufficient acidity, chemicals in the pesticide transformed into a toxic compound—name and molecular structure on the overhead—which in a high enough concentration in the human body blocked the absorption of these nutrients so that a person would, in effect, starve. No matter what she consumed.

This was the extraordinary thing to witness, the opposite of a miracle: meals were prepared daily with clean food and served to the afflicted, again in church basements (there were many) or school cafeterias. And yet, although the trays were full and then empty, the people sitting before us were disappearing, their faces hollowing, arms bearing the thick down of the emaciated, bellies swelling. The children ate pints of ice cream, bags of chips, entire cakes. Of course this is what charities preferred to send, food that contained so few nutrients, it hardly mattered that the body could make nothing of them—but these were the photographs broadcast all over, brown-skinned children, playground gangs of famine victims, digging at quarts of Neapolitan with plastic spoons. *Bizarre malady* was the phrase several news networks had settled upon. As though no one could have foreseen any of this, who could have known that, among the monstrosities of creation, this too might one day rise from the earth?

*GENVASO engages in frantic clean-up efforts*, the newspapers told us, or we told the newspapers. The strawberry plants were uprooted and sealed in plastic, awaiting determination as to whether it was safe to burn them, and where. The laborers responsible for the task wore suits like ours, and so moved very slowly, with an almost comical clumsiness—though I saw them only once, every time since then the security contractors had warned me off, and no one would allow us to interview them. We were assured that GENVASO was monitoring their safety with regular blood tests, and that their heroism would never be forgotten by the company, indeed by the nation, this we were informed almost daily. The fields were cut out in chunks of earth three feet deep, rocks hauled away.

Three feet being the depth beyond which, we were briefed, the pesticide would not permeate. This did not assuage doubts about the groundwater, and when a reservoir was tested then condemned, those in the county who had not already fled were evacuated. The songbirds, on cue, had lapsed into silence, their bodies to be found on sidewalks or disconcertingly on any path one might take toward the river to relieve one's mind in the dusk.

The toxin could be found in sweat and had come home from the fields borne on the skin of men and women to their children. Even as I sat, as had become my habit each afternoon, by the children in their cots in the medical center, I wore my suit; and so often I failed to understand their whispered words and heard only their cries. No one could say whether brief contact with their skin was sufficient exposure. We held their hands in the exaggerated plastic forms of our own. They held each other's bare hands, until they became too sick, and lay quietly, and no longer cried. I murmured the words to songs we'd sung during the strikes in the old days, sitting on the hot earth, workers getting arrested row by row, beaten with nightsticks, faces pressed to the topsoil. These songs were no lullaby, and if anyone passed near us I fell back into silence.

# ALICE

*T*hings I didn't tell Modigliani: I went up to the lake where Frances had crashed his motorcycle, a crash that would eventually lead him to the hospital room where his body was found. The local cops said, emphasis on the adverb, that officially the crash was an accident.

The flight was long and the drive from the airport two hours. Oh, it's beautiful up there, everyone behind any counter said.

I expected the lake to just stretch out before me, I'd look to the horizon and see only water. The blue was huge on the map, but the land laid its own claims. Spurs of evergreen forest interrupted the vista of water, behind them the shore rose into small hills, erratic boulders visible in the green. Evergreens everywhere. I took the lakeshore drive, which boasted more dinky hotels and condos but fewer strip malls. Every few miles a beach had been cut clear, sand trucked in, and a boardwalk of arcades, drink stands, varieties of tiki bars and balsa-wood night clubs gathered round. As far as I could tell the place was warm enough for swimming about six weeks a year. Little piers studded the shores, motorboats, jet skis, tons of fishing. You need a license to fish, the woman at the motel said, the cheapest motel I could find, which was incredibly cheap. But no one really cares, she said, anyway you can get one at Walmart.

Frances had crashed on a stretch of road between the

state bird preserve and one of the largest beaches. Houses were sparse here, a couple trucks or rusted chassis parked in each yard. In the woods every half-mile or so small ponds appeared and from the road I could see evidence of logging and glimpse men leading dogs to or from water. Frances had skidded out on one of the road's abrupt curves, where a long finger of lake pointed inland. It was raining, his mother had told me, but it's always raining that time of year.

I drove slowly. I guessed his skid must have taken him onto the dirt frontage road that shadowed the main route. I turned around, approached the scene again. I was driving so slowly that when a heron lifted off from a pond in the green we were for a moment moving at the same speed.

Frances had broken his right leg and a bunch else. He was wearing a helmet, but according to his brother this was only because he'd lost a bet. If I won the bet, the brother said, then Frances had to wear his helmet for a month.

I asked what the bet was, but he wouldn't tell me.

Frances's lower right leg had already been smashed in Iraq, two pins still in it. The new break had gotten very nasty because of this, which was one reason he'd ended up back in a big VA hospital, the new injury complicating the old. I'd go to his local VA hospital to follow up, though I'd already learned why he'd been flown out to the hospital where he died: this PTSD study was particular and he fit its criteria precisely. The accident completed, if you will, his dossier. And their physical therapy facilities were among the best in the country.

My father, Frances's grandfather, owned a lot of land

around here that got bought up for developments when I was a kid, Frances's mom said, by way of explanation: Then he invested it in Lockheed Martin, my dad, where he worked, so he did really well. So when it cost more to send Frances somewhere, well, we took care of him.

She had agreed to talk to me, but on her front porch, not in the house. I've just treated the carpets for fleas, she said, I don't want you breathing all that.

I couldn't argue, and complimented her on her irises. I didn't know they could grow so well so far north, I said.

She smiled briefly and tapped her nails on the porch railing.

I didn't stay long, and when I left I drove again along the road where Frances had nearly died. I pictured the early spring rain, thin panes of ice forming darkly on the lake. I pulled onto the dirt road and got out. When a loon cackled above me I was so scared that I had to laugh.

# OMAR

She says: watch carefully. She reaches over, does something on the keyboard and the clip restarts. Almost excited she says, it looks like he's—well, you'll see. Onscreen the shouting begins and the sound of popping. The camera is amateurish, everywhere, wild—faces, too close, mouths open, thighs, jeans and asses, shoulders, hands the guns are in. Beside the road is a slope, the camera descends—there is the mouth of the drainpipe and the man they pull out of it, blood already smeared mustache to chin. It looks like him, I say, it's definitely him, though I guess we can't know for sure. Wait, she says. Close around the man they're shouting and using the butts of their guns. The man is trying to speak. We don't know the language and couldn't have heard him over the shouting, prayers and gunfire popping. I read that he offered all the rebels gold and their children free education. This is it, she says, and hits the keyboard but the video doesn't slow, it speeds up. Shit, she says. She scrolls back. His back is to us and more than two men grip him, and another man, hand on the captured man's shoulder, seems to be holding something and thrusting, blood seeps through the captured man's pants. What is he holding? she asks, which is not what I was thinking. A machete? she asks, and scrolls back. The man's face is the face of the dictator, his expression unfamiliar. By the end of the video he appears to be dead. They are lifting him bloodied into the back of the truck, men surround him, the shouts praise God, one man grips the dictator's hair to nod his head up and down. He may not yet be dead. But by the next video he's naked from the waist up and we can see the gunshot wounds, then his body moves out of the range of the camera, dragged along the dirt. It looks like a stick or a machete, she says, right? You'll have to do a frame-by-frame, I say, it's too hard to tell. In the last still his head is tilted back, red smudged on the pouch of his chin, his eyes closed, nostrils deep and wide. All day people have been saying that it's a travesty, he should have been tried. He would have enjoyed a trial, others said, I think I was among them.

*I*t's not that Modigliani thinks he's always welcome, he's just always there. Haven't you already interviewed them? I said, meaning our victim Diana's sister and Diana's child, who was too young to talk. Her sister had at last agreed to talk to me. Sure, he said, they won't be happy to see me, the sister has a real mouth on her.

I nodded, tried to dissuade him, tried to change the appointment, failed. At least he offered to drive, or rather, he assumed that he'd drive. The town Diana's sister lived in was four hours away, in the undefined territory between the more populated northern and southern parts of the state, west of the mountains, an area I'd never thought about. The town was small but spread out thinly, and she lived down near the dam, close to the trailer parks but further up the state route, in a patch between strip malls where there was a real drive-in, as well as an antiques store, a dentist's office, and two gas stations across the street from each other, the one on the north side a few cents a gallon cheaper. We pulled into a long dirt driveway. In the yard were one of those elaborate plastic playhouses, a plastic kitchenette set, a three-wheeled wagon lying on its side, and two setups for T-ball. The house had a high concrete foundation and was oddly shaped, roof nearly touching the long grass on one side, on the other a porch, where a man in a hoodie and jeans was sitting and smoking, doing something with his phone. Modigliani laid his hand on my arm, and we were quite close to the man when Modigliani said, Good evening, and the man looked up, or rather down, since we were in fact below him, our faces visible only through the railing.

Jesus, he said.

We're looking for Cerise, Modigliani said.

Who the fuck are you? the man said.

Modigliani got out his identification and we introduced ourselves: Is it all right if—? Modigliani gestured toward the porch stairs, and we ascended.

We had an appointment to speak with Cerise, Modigliani said.

For tonight? the man put out his cigarette and slid his phone into his pocket.

At 6, I said.

He shook his head. She just went out, didn't say where she was going.

I confirmed with her yesterday, I said.

Guess she didn't want to talk to you, he said, and rose to jerk the sliding door open. A boy, about five, stood on the other side, braid of red licorice in his hand.

I told you not to leave your sister until the movie was over, the man said.

I have to pee, the boy said.

No, you just went, the man said. Go watch your movie.

Somewhere inside the house a child began crying.

Jesus, the man said, I told you not to leave your sister.

She's not my sister, the child said matter-of-factly, which I understood to mean that the girl must be Diana's. Lacey, two and a half.

Lacey! the man called into the house. Just a minute, he said to us, and stepped through the doorway, his hand on the boy's head as they walked. The boy's sweatpants were too long and he moved with a sort of shuffling slide. Modigliani and I waited, and the man returned holding a toddler who was screaming into his shoulder.

Over the noise he said: You guys can wait for Cerise on the porch, if you want, but I don't think she's coming back.

He was holding the girl but not soothing her, and she was wriggling fiercely, her T-shirt bunched up to expose her chest and stomach. The girl's skin was darker than her mother's was, and at the moment a small red lump was twisted up in her curls, presumably licorice.

Her diaper needs to be changed, Modigliani said.

I looked at the man to apologize, but he was looking past us, into the trees that bordered the yard.

Anything you want me to tell her? he said.

We just wanted to talk to her about Diana, I said, before Modigliani could answer.

The child was now facing us, her screaming full-throated. Do you want me to—I said, reaching out, but fortunately he didn't hear me.

She'll talk to you again when you've caught the guy, the man said to Modigliani. She won't talk to any reporters, he said, now looking at me, and you better not print anything, or what you'll learn about the Robarge girls is how they lose their fucking tempers. That girl's got lawyers on speed dial, you don't want to see it.

Understood, I said. Modigliani didn't say anything, just slid the glass door open for the man and child to pass through.

We walked back to the car, the sky above the trees along the property line pinking.

We stopped at the more expensive gas station and headed back, a bag of sunflower seeds propped up between us.

Supposedly Diana went into rehab for drinking last summer, Modigliani said. For a month or so. The daughter's been living with the sister ever since. The story is, Diana got out of rehab, relapsed, and then eventually went to the VA hospital for another course of treatment, this time focusing on her PTSD. But we can't find any rehab facility it seems plausible she could have gone to—no record of her anywhere around here, including the place she told her sister she was at, and in any case they're all out of her price range.

Hmm, I said, although I already knew this. I already knew some ways to take a month when you needed a month. I asked: Does the family know she never went to rehab?

Modigliani shrugged. Who knows, he said—which if you think about it was exactly the question.

She could have used a fake name, he said.

But he must know that I'd checked every name.

She came back, though, I said. She must have wanted to come back, see her kid.

Sort of, he said, I mean, she was still drunk, then she went to live in a hospital.

Still, I said. She wanted to.


On the drive back I asked Modigliani: Did I tell you about Jonathan's dream?

Modigliani shook his head, facing the rain and the taillights which each sweep of the wiper blades sharpened then softened.

His girlfriend told me, I said, his ex-girlfriend. She's with someone new now, a contractor, she said, mostly kitchens, high-end. I talked to her twice, and the second time, when the new boyfriend wasn't there, she asked me, what did the doctor say about Jonathan's dream? What dream? I asked. She got angry, she said, I bet he didn't even tell anyone, I told him he should tell a doctor, maybe someone could help. She was crying through the whole interview, but her makeup never ran, her mascara was beyond belief. She said Jonathan had been having the dream for years, that it used to wake him up, and she'd ask but he wouldn't say anything about it, until one night he did—although she wasn't sure then whether to believe him, since they'd been just about to have a big fight when he interrupted in order to tell her his dream start to finish.

He said: I'm walking along a highway. There are dates in my pockets, I can feel the sticky paper of their skin and am gripping them, I don't want them to be loose in my pockets. Around me it's all desert, mice are running over the dunes, I can see them everywhere, constant motion. On the side of the road an old man in a checkered head-scarf is digging. There is another shovel, but I don't help him, I suspect that whoever was last holding that shovel is dead. As he digs he exposes what looks like a small city, a minaret extends bone-white out of the sand, and he keeps digging around it, his head bent very low. A truck stops for me and I get on. The truck is full of Iraqi policemen, and they're jumping off one by one. At first I think that they're running around to the front of the truck and climbing up again, but this isn't what's happening. One of them is shaking up cans of Coke and replacing them in the crate he's sitting on. I ask if I can help. I don't mean with the Coke, but he laughs, and when I look down, I see I am wearing not my uniform but the blue uniform of the Iraqi police, and the outlines of my fingers and the lines of my palms are thickening, like they were drawn in crayon. In the truck they are now speaking a language I don't speak, not even Arabic, it's some gibberish they've made up just because they don't want me to understand. I hear them say *Susanne* (and this, I tell Modigliani, is the name of Jonathan's ex-girlfriend, the one who is telling me the dream), and I reach for one of the guns along the side of the truck, but they laugh and push me out the back. I land hard in the middle of a city square. The building walls are covered in graffiti and posters and in the square's center there's a fountain, which has no water, and next to it a young man is cooling an overheated car. The man's face is the same as the face on a poster behind him, which I think means that he's supposed to be dead. I walk over to him and one of his children runs up to me, sticks out a hand and asks for money. I reach into my pockets, but my pockets are dark with blood, as if dates could bleed. It doesn't occur to me to wonder about my legs. The man by the hood of the car watches me, then he nods at the child. I believe that the man is going to kill me, and in the window of the car I see my face lost in darkness. I'm worried about whoever is in the car, that they'll have to see what happens next, and I wake up.

She told you all that? Modigliani said.

Yes, I said, I recorded her and I've listened many times.

I don't think it's the real dream, though, I said. I think there's another dream.

# MARIE

At night the door to the study was always closed. The cat would wait outside it and I couldn't let the cat get in. Mess everything about. There weren't even piles, really—rather documents and photographs fanned out over the table, as if I were a child learning magic tricks, these my cards. I wish I could say that every morning I had to force myself to enter. That I would scrub the kitchen counters, prepare next week's lecture, walk to the corner mailbox, anything to delay. No: I rose early, made up a French press and with my elbow opened the door. I knew the location of every item on the table, could reach without looking, and it was now my daily regret that I had not made of the table's array a facsimile of the actual geography—monks to the west, monastery in the hills; here the village; the road; here the military base. My computer was positioned so that while I wrote I could see not the table but out the window, past the lightning-struck oak to the row of hemlocks, and to my left was my old shelf of reference books, which the internet had made quaint, a scholarly flourish.

I had thought to begin the next chapter with the monks, but now that too seemed a facile trope: austere withdrawal from the world; the world's violent reclamation. What profit another retelling of the old story, the defeat of faith, treachery of God? I should confront the fate of the monks with a more radical judgment—who, after all, should think that he may retreat from the world, forswear desire, the world's very lifeblood, turn his face toward God yet away from His accursed creation? I would begin the chapter in the village with a portrait not of faith or its tribulations, but of pure endurance: two young women had survived the massacre by hiding on a rooftop, one of the only flat roofs in the village, with a knee-high sort of façade wall shielding them from view of the men below. I didn't know the architectural word for this wall and it was proving irritatingly difficult to discover. And should I use words that would send the reader to the dictionary (and then email; and then the news…)?—accuracy less important than avoiding distraction. In their accounts survivors of such events always talk about how they could hear the screaming, how the screaming haunts them. But rarely does anyone mention what was said; or perhaps this detail is in its tragic mundanity always the first thing trimmed from the interview, the translation. They were crying out to God, one of the girls on the rooftop had said. The girls must have heard pleas, heard the names of children. Some of the men could have been known to their victims. Their victims might have called them by name. Perhaps memory washes out the words, leaves only the sound of screaming, which seems like the brain's sort of kindness. The men arrived at the monastery bloodied from the slaughter of the village. Another reason not to begin with the monks: they got to live at least this short time longer. And in theory didn't they lose the least of their lives—a single breath, these days on earth, compared with the eternity to come? Standing over the table I turn over the photographs, which I keep face down, out of an idea of sensitivity. But I can look at them now while eating a sandwich; I can see them on closing my eyes. I've been like this for years.

It took years to find even one man who might that day have been among the killers in the village, who might have been known by someone to belong to the rebel forces who kept at first to the mountains, and then—and then this. An eye expelled from its socket; a boot print in a woman's head. The photographs were taken more than a day after the massacre, when the first journalists arrived on the scene. Or, properly, the only journalists—an Agence France-Presse reporter and a locally born photographer. Two years later the reporter would be dead, killed by fundamentalist thugs who were purging the capital of foreigners. I had not found the photographer; no one had. The AFP editor would tell me nothing, saying that in those days for the employees' own protection they used none of the locals' real names. In the photographs the blood is darkened, but there is not yet any real decay, only in some a massing of insects and the effects of heat and the body's desiccation. Ant tracks of blood cross this woman's shin, which in death her dark robe has bunched up to expose, in life it would not have been seen outside the walls of her home. Though I should not say that, truly I know nothing of her, her measure of zealousness or its many opposites. She died on the doorstep, her family within, the cuts on her arms what are called defensive wounds. No real forensic evaluation was done—it is only that through the years many, like me, have studied the photographs and the accounts. Many have been interested in the monks, especially the monks; there had been a monastery on this site for 150 years, each article notes. As though this were an important detail, or anyone couldn't know that this meant only: since the advent of colonialism. The monks were foreigners, and for this reason if they could have been killed twice, they would have been. They were good to the village, it was said, sharing of their garden's surplus and supplying medical care, although since they were untrained one wonders what that might have meant. The militia slaughtered the monastery's sheep as well as its men. The chickens were either killed or escaped; there were none in the photograph of the aftermath. This photograph was shot from a distance: the bodies of the monks and the animal carcasses had been heaped and set alight. But had not burned completely, and the smell must have kept even this courageous photographer at a remove; or perhaps it was simply that none of his shots from close up were good enough to develop. And now the cat is at my ankles, rubbing her cheeks against me with the likeness of affection that is an expression of scent glands. I had gathered the names of everyone in the village, but not the name of the photographer, who might still be alive. I should say, I had 138 names, which I believed to be everyone in the village—although I might not know if someone had escaped; or if one of the young men among the killers was also one of the young men from the village, and thus had survived.

A generation: boys became men who joined one side or the other. In the name of God butchering foreigners, professors, women who worked outside the home, infidels, anyone, it came to be, throats slit so deep the spine was visible. Or, on the other side, the army and police manning the torture chambers, pulling thousands of so-called suspects and their families out of mosques, off the streets, out of their homes and into the darkness where thousands would then die. It had taken years to find the name I'd been looking for, the name we all knew must exist but could not conjure, many had theorized but I had now found: one man who was both on the payroll of the army and a leader in the rebel forces. He had led the forces into this village, dispatched ten men to the monastery. I had found him. And in this book he would be made known. Forgive me my pride. I won't use the word *payroll*; that no one could establish absolutely, but a man who had been arrested, tortured, then released, curiously never to be bothered again, and through the years was seen meeting with other army informants, even, repeatedly, with two officers, all the while ascending the ranks of the rebels, having manned the infamous checkpoint on the mountain road where at the beginning of the conflict five aid workers had been murdered and then the thirteen soldiers sent for them, the irrevocable act of war. For years I had tracked him. People call what one follows the scent, but I—who have spent so long with these photographs, stench ever absent from them, from the human forms they document—I would not use that word. He was an idea whose incarnation I had discovered, the man I had if not made flesh, brought to light.

This massacre was his work, by the time of these photographs he was gone from the hills, from the dirt floors on which the dead were laid, but it is as though on looking long enough one sees a spectral evidence. How often have I envisioned you, through the window the hemlocks in frost and thaw. Everyone knew that there had been no shortage of collaborators, on both sides. Anyone anywhere would say that the army had been dirty. But, they always added, always the absolution: it was a dirty fight, against an enemy monstrous beyond imagining, the massacre of the village only one example of its terror and in many ways not the worst. And yet—this village was low in the foothills and the military base was in the valley right below, quite close, would not the sounds have carried? The hours of screaming to which those two women could testify? Tragically, everyone at the base had been out that day, responding to another incident, the base commander had said, and his logs verified. But now, here, I had a name, a man to prove that the army was its own enemy, dirtied the fight itself, while the aid money rolled in, and better than aid money, the guns. I had no image of him and I had to imagine a face, unbearded, suspended in the evening light past my reflection. That country which had stepped through the looking glass: shaven fundamentalists and ski-masked police.

*In that country*, I would write, *out of the hills, the torture chambers, ghettos and far-flung villages, training camps and officer schools, a new nation of man was born, in one body terrorist and soldier.* Now he walks among us, coffers filling and mothers throwing up their arms in the doorways. I see those girls, cheeks pressed to the hot slate, no doubt their skin burning, and for hours rising toward them every cry from below. For a moment the screams are my name; they cry out my name.

Do not forgive me, but this is the thought that permits me, each day, to sit down at the desk and begin.

# ALICE

*Back in a few days*, I texted Modigliani. *Text me if you crack the case.*

I flew north, dozing on the plane with my head tipped back—my neck, I kept thinking, exposed. In my dreams I was on an airplane, the man beside me shuffling and re-shuffling a pinochle deck (not so—he too was sleeping, detective fiction in his lap), below us the Pacific Coast, green and foggy, even from this height you could see the surf, lacing around rocks, the shore a soft pastureland dotted with sheep and hikers. When I woke I could see out the window a glaciered peak emerging from cloud.

Sergei's parents had wanted to meet in a popular tourist spot, maybe they thought it would be easiest for me to find. I took the train downtown from the airport, gliding past small hills, urban trailer parks, long blocks of the Vietnamese neighborhood. I got off and walked downhill toward the harbor, on the horizon a blur of islands across the sound. I hadn't been to this city in ten years but the people were all familiar. Everywhere they passed with what seemed like an air of geniality, as though they all knew each other too well to look up and say hello. The city was getting richer and richer but the business district was just a few blocks that appeared discreetly then melted back into the slope of little neighborhoods and rows of condos down toward the bay.

Then the historic market sign was before me, and

since I was early I entered the press of tourists as they moved leisurely through the stalls, easily wooed to either side by fishmongers, cheap jewelers, florists. The crabs the fishmongers pointed to were indeed immense, and the bouquets, while ordinary, were glorious in the misty air. I bought some sort of honey candy and sucked on it as I made my way to the piroshky stand, which is where Sergei's family had wanted to meet, whether out of sincere enthusiasm or a sense of humor I didn't know. We had only exchanged emails, and even that with much delay and confusion—the two of them shared an address and checked it infrequently; I imagined that they had acquired it solely to talk to Sergei when he was overseas.

*He sent little videos*, they'd written to me. *Of him and a boy he was teaching English. Rap songs, them singing together.* They'd tried to embed one but the link was broken.

The line at the piroshky stand was long, and no one in it looked like his parents as I had pictured them. These were tourists, intent on the display, where pastries shone with egg wash, the poppy seed fillings looked as rich as caviar, and the curves of the rolls were enormous, so that it would take two hands even to hold one of these creations, and an hour to eat them, if instead of biting through you unspooled the spiral as it had been formed. Piroshkies, hot in waxed paper, were handed over the counter again and again, and briefly I was transfixed by the vigor of the teenage staff, one handling dough adeptly, one hurrying to and from the back, others taking and filling orders as if the security camera above us was intended to document their professionalism.

The stand was a few doors down from the original Starbucks, and a parade of people posed by its quaint proto-logo, their companions taking their photographs, and then switching places, continually disrupting the foot traffic. Do you mind...? two young women asked me, one of them offering her phone and gesturing toward the sign. Her friend held an oversized bouquet.

Sorry, I said, my hands in my pockets. The women took it better than most.

I walked a short distance from the bustle and waited. Sergei's parents were now ten minutes late. I had given them my cell number but they had not done the same. I had described myself well enough, I thought, looking down at my jacket. The crowd made this a poor choice of places to meet, and why had I agreed to it?

Once they were half an hour late, I got in line for a piroshky, still looking around, which made the middle-aged mother behind me nervous. I ordered the mushroom, potato, and cabbage. The filling was exceptional, the pocket firm. I walked a bit farther, to finish eating while looking at the harbor, thinking of ships' bellies packed with immigrants, the bravery of those who had made the crossing, a courage so necessary it was almost mundane. I waited another hour, one eye on the stand and checking email on my phone too often. Perhaps they wanted to meet here so that when they stood me up I'd at least see the city, I thought, and left. I headed perpendicular from my hotel, figuring I now had the afternoon for as long a walk as I wanted, could even work in a couple of the city's bridges, look down and see past my feet the long drop to the water.

The sun came out and I walked for hours, ending stretched out in the grass of a small park. Two men drowsed, holding hands, a few yards from me, their stereo murmuring old-school hip-hop. When a man, good-looking, not too young, stopped to talk to me—after returning a piece of paper that he thought had blown free from my notebook—I was friendly. This city, I thought, following him to the neighborhood bar he recommended, where the beer selection was as good as he'd claimed, and we ate plates of kale and macaroni and cheese. I wasn't surprised that he kissed me, but was surprised that it was on the street, where a woman sitting on a stoop two buildings over could catcall. When it turned out his apartment wasn't far from my hotel I went with him. I came easily, his fingers at once in me and rubbing me, we kissed half-undressed in his room, not yet in his bed but leaning against an armoire. After that I didn't think about anything. I didn't stay, I had called my hotel from the bathroom, to say I would be late but still keeping my reservation. Next to the light switch in the bathroom—so that as I sat his face appeared above mine in the mirror opposite, and he'd have gazed at your chest if you stood to pee—was a framed photograph of Frantz Fanon. I didn't comment on this when I came back to bed, though from my companion's expression I think he was hoping I would; he could have assumed I hadn't noticed the portrait, or didn't know who it was.

*I*'d heard Mahatma was here, there, everywhere. Every-one said something different. *I just saw him, like down MLK Boulevard.*

*It's just him, by the bridge, in front of all these cops, he's just standing there talking and they won't say shit back.*

*I saw him standing guard over a cop car so this kid wouldn't smash its windows, blocking him, just like talking him down.*

*He's under a tree on the north side of the park, giving a speech, you should have heard him...*

*I saw him where the fire's at, throwing tear gas right back at them.*

Everything was possible, could be nothing was true. I did what I knew how to do. Zipped a hoodie to my chin, tied a kerchief snug across my face. My press pass slapped at my gut as I passed through the crowd, men women and children peaceably assembled, signs high in the fouled air. On every T-shirt a single face appeared, a young man, eyebrows low in thought or bemusement, half his face in shadow, half in sun. In the original photo his T-shirt was red, the background red brick, here reproduced in black and white—T-shirt on a T-shirt, I thought, ha, not an in-finite regression, but close enough: everywhere I turned, he gazed at me through the obstructed light of the street, inquiring, silent.

This man, Ferdinand, had died two weeks before the protests began. Protests that were now, officially, riots. In my mother's living room I'd perched on the arm of the couch and watched dozens of boys and men, some women, yes, some women in there, sifting rapidly in and out of a check cashing store, *a horde*, they said on the news, narrating fast over helicopter footage, from that height there were just dark bodies and white T-shirts, not one face. The faster the newscasters talked the calmer I felt. My mother walked by and smacked at my rear: That's not how a couch works and you know it. When I packed my knapsack in the hall, still chewing toast, she handed me the kerchief and a water bottle with a squeeze top. There's all that tear gas out there, she said. I raised my eyebrows, and she said: You kids think you're the only ones ever been worth gassing. She brushed something invisible off my sleeve and I was out the door.

You know Mahatma? I asked the men lined up protecting a corner store, street soldiers, tough and coughing. Yeah, man, one of them said and they conferred for a moment then told me where he was, where I was soon to learn he wasn't. Can I get a photo? I said, of you all together, and I gestured at the kerchiefs they were wearing, half of which were red, half blue, testimony to the truce the gangs had called for the protests. I tried to get them arranged in that tight line, in the window behind them the face of the shopkeeper, but one or two were always doubled over coughing, alternately, a sort of choir. The man I talked to, blue kerchief at his throat, shouted after me as I walked away, and when I turned back toward him I saw the capillaries in his left eye give, the white flooded red. When you find Mahatma, he said, tell him we'll do what he asked. What did he ask? I said, like a goddamn reporter. Nah, man, he said. Just tell him.

Two weeks ago Ferdinand had died. Three weeks ago Ferdinand had seen a couple cops on the street and the cops had seen him, for a second they'd looked at each other, then Ferdinand turned and ran. Cops in hot pursuit. When they caught him they arrested him, though since they were lacking any cause this event falls in that dissonant category termed *unlawful arrests*. They hauled him to a police van, his leg dragging, broken, his dragging leg and cries of pain attracting the camera phone of a passerby, who shouted at the cops, while another man filmed from another angle (*I went around to the back of the building when I heard the sound of the taser*, he said later, *they had him folded up like a crab*). In the video the heels of Ferdinand's sneakers tilt up from his shoulder blades, the two police officers' hands pressing hard on his shoulders and shins. It was in the van that three of his vertebrae were crushed, his head nearly loose from his spine, there on the floor he lost consciousness; he was shackled to himself but loose in the van. For a week he endured, unspeaking, until one morning he died.

The city is getting louder. The morning is warm and sirens approach and recede, a sonar that fails to locate the hot heart of the city. Mahatma? I ask, and people point, people nod. Down the street a stolen car luxuriates in slow circles before a wall of riot cops, their plastic-shielded gaze. I want at once to be deeper in and more peripheral. The emcee is my answer, the city's best known, Mahatma, and I'll—I'll smoke him out, I could say, given the skies under which we both find ourselves, the air we're barely able to breathe.

Only once had Mahatma appeared on the news, his lawyer beside him, by chance one of his hearings had been amid the first days that the protests transformed into whatever it was they'd become. On the courthouse steps they stopped him, mikes raised, and he had already rolled up the sleeves of his button-down, his tie pendulating when he answered first one reporter, then the next. His tie matched so precisely the sky that he looked transparent, or sliced through, atmosphere itself radiating from his breastbone. His lawyer wore a tight-fitting suit, a sort of '60s Bob Dylan tribute that looked somehow cynical, perhaps only because a phone was glowing through the front pocket. A reporter began: *It seems like the nonviolent protest you called for has failed.* I guess it seems like that, Mahatma said, and paused artfully, but the reporter—blonde in a kelly-green wrap dress—only went on: *What message would you like to give to the looters?* As though her mike were a means to address them. Well, he said, I believe in nonviolence, but—he looked off into the distance, a gaze his lawyer suddenly joined, like two deer upon hearing a crack in the woods—the master's tools will never dismantle the master's house. I waited for him to go on, but when someone then asked him about his own hearing, the charges he'd been contesting for over a year, he replied formulaically and his lawyer stepped in. *We may have just heard*, the blonde thought aloud to the camera, *one of the city's most prominent figures, the rapper Mahatma, endorse the rioting. Let's go to*—and when the head of the usual reverend pundit appeared I hit mute. Briefly the photo of Ferdinand occupied the screen.

Everywhere I went Mahatma had been. We need his leadership now more than ever, a woman said, and a boy, no more than thirteen, played me a recording he'd made of one of Mahatma's impromptu performances, but any song was indistinct from the rising noise of the street. The streak of red across the boy's shirt seemed to come from the crown of his head, he wiped a new trickle away from his lips.

*If he's not talking to the media*, my editor texted me, *what makes you think you're any different?* I had paused in a barricaded street to read this when I was arrested, thrown forward into a junked-out car and handcuffed, painfully. I'm a—I said, but it seemed like nobody heard me, and although I should have gone limp I guess I helped walk myself to the van. Just then Mahatma was on the corner ahead, a crowd gathering to him, I saw him raise his hand to his face, with a knuckle rub the smoke and damp from his eyes.

*I*t was not a good bar, but Modigliani seemed to like it, we had been there almost three hours. His head was tipped back against the wall, his Adam's apple a pearl in the yellow light. In my jacket pocket was the envelope Kareem's wife Simone had sent me, of which I said nothing to Modigliani. I planned to read it that night and was careful not to get too drunk, a restraint in which Modigliani decidedly did not share.

I called him a cab and he walked toward it shaking his head, his only farewell a hand on my arm that could have been merely for balance. I went home—no longer the hotel but a shitty efficiency on the seventh floor of a shitty compound. From the kitchen window I could see the roof of the VA hospital, a view I had thought would help keep my head in the game.

Rubber-banded around the contents of the envelope was a note: *I thought you should have this. Not the police.* I didn't know if the sentence fragment signified afterthought or emphasis. Simone had signed it with an S and a sketch of a cat.

When I removed the rubber band, papers fell to the bedspread and floor. Various documents, notes on pages torn from a notebook, newspaper printouts, a CD labeled *backup.* This seemed like Kareem's mess, not Simone's, as though she'd sent me the disordered contents of a drawer or the stereotypical shoebox.

I dug in.

The main theme so far: a prison in Afghanistan, which I'd heard of but never been anywhere near. Before Iraq Kareem had served two years in Afghanistan, if I remembered right—one of the spiral-bound pages told me this, actually, in his tidy handwriting he'd written the dates and sites of his deployments and a few select missions, with more geographical specificity than seemed strictly kosher.

Kareem was not a man of sentences, which I respected. His notes were lists, with arrows and circles, dates and names whose relation was suggested by their situation on the page. Everywhere the initials FAM—by the name of a village, the date of what? It seems they had encountered FAM on the road. A checkpoint, where FAM had been dragged out of the taxi he drove.

The prison was the subject of the next stack of newspaper printouts, which I had to smooth out to read, the creases in them deep and irregular, they'd been folded into small triangles, or maybe stuffed in a pocket, and although one might have called Kareem a slob, he had instead, I thought, a cynical sort of order, in which treasures were deliberately disguised as trash. The prison was in the mountains, at first just a temporary holding pen, a place to collect and interrogate while the war tried to sort out the young men of the north, their affiliations and those of the local warlords, but now, years later, it was overfull, and the articles—which were several years old—expressed the beginnings of the present concern that there was no due process of any kind at work here. The so-called worst of the worst were shipped to Guantanamo; others disappeared behind these walls for years or forever.

The death certificate was a photocopy and in English. Across the top Kareem had written: *rec'd by FAM's family 2/1*. The certificate recorded the January 7, 2003, homicide of Farzad Ahmad Muhammad, *coronary failure due to blunt force injury*—this phrase highlighted in yellow.

The rest was: a list of names, American military, ordered by rank, and all stationed, it seemed, in the prison, though I'd have to look into that further. I clicked through the files on the CD, which, as the label promised, were only scans of the hard copies, often blurry, marred by the documents' creases and of little use. This was neither evidence nor argument, but inchoate, its purpose known only to Kareem. Had any one of these items been discovered among his things it would have raised no particular interest, which was no doubt his aim. And Simone, who must have understood the man's mind, what did she think upon discovering all this? That she wanted someone else to deal with it? Although (I looked at a photo of FAM, an impromptu mug shot, his hands plastic handcuffed, expression frightened, his face young, thin, thinly bearded, robes billowing wide of his ankles, to each side of him a GI, one of whom was smiling incongruously) that wasn't fair. She would like to honor his inquiry, or interest, whatever it was. As well as to have the weight of it off her shoulders, out of her house, which she must by now be selling. I was in Iraq, I had said to her, as a sort of persuasion so that she might tell me more, we stood in her living room, her eyes flicking toward the room where the child slept whenever I spoke or a car passed throbbing with music.

And tonight, among the things spread over my bed: a photograph of Simone and the boy as a newborn. It could be that this was Kareem's, stored for safekeeping with his amateur investigation; or Simone may have enclosed it, meaning it for me.

The next day when I saw Modigliani I said: Does the name Farzad Ahmad Muhammad mean anything to you?

He shook his head.

I'm sure he'd have asked me to elaborate, but at that moment our breakfasts arrived, Modigliani's toast burned and mine nicely browned. I smiled at him. Can we get some more orange juice? Modigliani asked the waitress. When she returned with two glasses he didn't thank her, and my mouth was full.

I had a dream last night, Modigliani said, slicing off a burned crust. About bison, tons of bison. Charging, not toward me, but past me, in a way. There was something ahead, something dangerous, that I wanted to warn them about. But how do you warn a pack of bison?

Herd, I said.

What?

A herd of bison.

He shook his head and in that common but embarrassing way we reached for our juice at the same time.

Do you think, I asked, that you actually even know what a charging bison looks like? In your conscious mind, you probably don't, you can't picture it, but maybe somewhere you've seen it, and when you dream you remember. That's what I've always wondered about. With dreams, I mean.

I don't know, he said.

You were probably still drunk, I said.

I woke up with a real headache, he said. He flicked his coffee cup with a fingernail, one exquisite chime.

Do you think it was a cliff? he asked. The thing in the distance?

Maybe, I said. Or just a ranch fence, that would be enough.

He paused and I thought that would be the end of it, but then he said: When I was a kid, I used to go for these walks along the riverbed of the Ohio. There's the river and then this stretch between the water and the land, all rocks and muck and driftwood, which floods when they open the dam, or just in flood season. I collected driftwood. I think someone had told me that you could make furniture with it. There are all these fossils in the rocks there. You're just walking over them the whole time. It's not like other places, where you'll be walking and see a fossil, great—it's like whole rock faces are just fossil. I used to walk bending over to look at them.

He pushed his balled-up napkin beneath the edge of his plate: There were bison there back in the day, everywhere, that's what they said. There was a big stuffed one in the visitor center by the river, where you could go get a soda or whatever. So when I walked along all bent over, I used to picture a bison watching me from the trees on the bank. Waiting to come down to the water. I wouldn't turn around, that was the deal. If I turn around, you know, it's not there.

Sure, I said.

Every time they opened the dam, there'd be a siren, then you had fifteen minutes to clear out, get to high ground. All the fisherman, kids like me, whoever was down by the water. We'd hear the siren but act real relaxed about it, I didn't want to run for it in front of the fisherman or the guys who got drunk down there, so I'd just turn and walk fast but normal toward the bank. It didn't take long to get high enough up, there was always plenty of time. But what I was thinking back then was, the bison don't know what the siren means.

They'd hear the water, I said, and they're fast.

Whatever, Modigliani said, I didn't know that then.

We didn't say anything for a bit, heaped up singles and coins on the bill, not really counting, or at least I wasn't. Let God sort 'em out, I said, adding a last quarter.

We left, and as Modigliani held open the door he pulled out a pack of cigarettes.

I didn't know you smoked, I said.

You're better than I am, he said belatedly, with names.

Faces I remember a while, he added. But what really gets me—he tapped the pack on his forearm then opened it—is a good turn of phrase.

He lit my cigarette then his own. The day was warming and we slid off our jackets.

# LA GRINGA

To think that Ivan had arranged a trip to my grand-mother's village just for me—I was touched. Ever since I had accepted a position on Ivan's staff, I'd kept in my wallet a photograph of my grandmother, a girl in her village. Anyone could see it when I opened my wallet at a café, for example, or a newspaper stand. Behind my back they still called me La Gringa. So I had to remind them, my grandmother was a peasant from these mountains—the very mountains you can see from anywhere in this city, whenever it's cool enough or bright enough that the haze and smog clear. I reminded them that one of the most insidious violations of colonialism was to force the poor to desert their own lands and flee into the arms of the colonizers. Beg for crumbs in an empire made rich off the spoils of their own lands. I'd have said this to anyone who challenged me. But my work speaks for itself and no one said a word, never to my face.

I met with Ivan almost daily, usually with his press secretary or foreign relations staff, though sometimes alone. Of course I disagreed with his restrictions on the press, and I did object, continually. His distrust, however, was only a further malignant consequence of neoimperialism. If he had not maintained rigorous defenses, foreign money would once again have flooded the newspapers until they printed libels about him, called for reelection, and when that did not suffice, fomented coup. Everyone remembered those years, me especially. I had been a complete novice—I'd come to this country only for work in medical translation, my first profession—but had I not traced this funding dollar by dollar back to the coffers of the CIA? From the bank accounts of three news services and a handful of think tanks and so-called charities? This must be remembered whenever people spoke of Ivan's suppression of press freedom. The so-called ideals of the (need I say, white, slave-owning) American founders were pretty selectively applied in the postcolonial reality. A foreign power was working to undermine a sovereign nation's government and civic society from within. The newspapers were not only not independent, but were corrupted to the core. I had seen the ledgers (in some cases, literally). When you are dealing with an opponent of endless wealth and minimal scruples, an opponent with a history of violently subjugating the people not only of this country but all over the world, the leashes of its attack dogs held by the cold hands of the oil corporations, you defend yourself by all means available. Ivan's ideological compromises with regard to the press were unfortunate, regrettable, and even, and I would use this word, offensive; but—and this was not only my hope but my aim—they would prove temporary.

I—just an amateur then, a hobby journalist—had been the very first to present hard evidence of the CIA's role in the coup attempt, the damning documents I had discovered and translated (translated literally and in the larger sense, so that everyone could read the writing on the wall). The money trail leading back to the steps of the White House, the umbilical cord of the most monstrous regimes of the South, of all the dictators who had handed over to American corporations the keys to the vaults of their countries—having horded away fortunes for themselves—and let the privatization begin. Not here. Ivan had defeated the coup and we would show the Americans that a country could thrive on their very doorstep not only resisting US influence but wielding no small influence of its own. A friend to every people's republic in the South.

Ivan had turned to me after a meeting last week and said, You have grown up from your American roots, but let us now have a look at the rest of your family tree.

Yes? I said.

I am going up into the mountains for the opening of one of our new water treatment plants, he said, I would like you to join me. Don't you carry with you a photograph of your grandmother? he gestured toward my purse. I have often noticed it, he said, it is very beautiful. What a beautiful woman, you can see everything in her face—he gestured again and I understood that I should find him the photograph, which I did—yes. He smiled and handed it back to me. Of course you look very much like her. She has your determination—or rather the grandmother of your determination, yes? Yours is much more. But this region, that is where I am going, I know the villages there well. You will travel with me. For me it will all be ceremonies and meetings, but you can take a car into the mountains and get to know her people. It is extraordinary there, like no place else—I'm sure she has told you. The air has a very unusual smell, there is nothing like it. Like goats and this kind of bush that only grows that high, it has deep pink blossoms and is used to make tea which is said to be good for the blood.

He leaned back and, as was his habit, twice smoothed the lap of his suit.

127

We'll go Thursday morning, he said, and return that night. And then on Saturday, you will attend the reception for Citizen Saeed. He is here for three days, and there will be meetings and a few things for show—he waved a hand in the air, which meant he had finished speaking. I rose, shook his hand, and kissed him on both cheeks, as he liked—the epicenter of the kiss, as it were, occurring not on his cheek proper but a few millimeters off, where his beard might have been after a few days' growth. Though I have always known him to be clean-shaven.

We departed for the mountains early Thursday morning. Ivan did not accompany me all the way to my grandmother's village, and I'd had no reason to think he would. He would meet with the administrators of the water treatment plant and hold the press conference, and I would be driven forty kilometers further into the mountains. Talk to the people there, he said, you will come to know your grandmother better, and he patted my hand.

The village was much as one would expect, though the background of mountains and sky more spectacular than I could have imagined. The children's clothes were not traditional but dirtied American castoffs—Mickey Mouse, Adidas, mesh shorts. Their feet were bare. Women cooked and chatted, the kitchens were tables under trees, plastic bowls arranged and a fire a few yards away. The dogs were like the dogs that had figured in my grandmother's stories, though the three-legged ringleader she had told us of was of course long dead. I had seen many such villages, the chickens, the dirt yards, dirty water, bad teeth— my grandmother had spoken often of her tooth pain as a child, and for this reason I was never to make fun of her poorly fitting bridge. The bush Ivan had described was everywhere, its blossoms a remarkable crimson, which as I bent to smell them seemed to throb with the headache I still always felt in the thin air.

I gave bread and sweets to the children, and would have played soccer with them, but they were shy. I talked to two of the old women, their speech thickly accented with the mountain tongue, which I did not speak. Could the driver translate, I wondered, but he was asleep, a newspaper laid over his face. The women did not seem to recognize the name of my grandmother, and there was no one else old enough to ask.

But the whole drive back—rubbing one of those flowers between my fingers, it looked somehow like brilliant miniature viscera—wasn't it true that I didn't think of my grandmother, not once, but of Citizen Saeed's imminent visit? This is the blessing and curse of work like mine: the mind never rests. In the car (he had requested that I move vehicles to join him) Ivan had said, In time the water-treatment plants will bring running water to each of these villages. It will take a few more years. But soon, he said, soon the first members of our new corps of teachers and nurses will be trained, and we will expand the schools and medical centers to serve even the most isolated rural areas. Already we have changed forever the lives and opportunities of those in the foothills, whom every government before us abandoned.

I knew this, of course, and no doubt this was language from his speech, but I didn't mind. He looked tired, the small pouch of skin beneath his chin jiggling as we descended the steep unpaved roads in the dark.

Soon, I said.

He opened his eyes at me, smiled. Try to sleep, he said, it is such a long drive to the airport.


I was prepared for Citizen Saeed to look small in person, which was usually the case when you met men you were used to seeing in the news—the greatest villains of our times, at least this was what the Western media bayed. Saeed, though, was quite tall. His dye job was as absurd as was reported.

It was strange to think that I had been a child when I first knew of him. A group unfortunately associated with his regime had perpetrated one of the world's first passenger-plane bombings, and I still remembered the newspaper photos, pieces of airliner falling like feathers to the sea. The Indian Ocean, was it? I do not think my memory of the photographs is accurate, though I held this image in me for a time as a child, not wishing even to fly with my mother to visit her brother in Florida (though of course eventually I did go). Saeed had been young then, though we in the West would describe his hairstyle as a decade behind. Back then he mostly wore military uniforms and his epaulets were exaggerated, so that his waist seemed particularly slim, and you might, if you were as young as I was, have confused him with David Bowie. Not a mistake anyone would make now.

Saeed met with Ivan's administration for a day that provided regular photo opportunities of them shaking hands and embracing in front of arrangements of the two flags. Ivan had been to visit Saeed six months before, this a follow-up to make further progress on their energy initiatives. As the US media was no doubt decrying even this minute, the two nations' alliance on issues in the international oil market might have real effect. I attended the teatime reception on the second day, among other members of Ivan's staff and a range of dignitaries and representatives of Ivan's youth leadership and rural women's education programs. Saeed rose to greet each of the women, though with decreasing effort, so that by the time I entered the room, he did little more than shift in his seat. Saeed and I had no language in common; Ivan had told me, he can speak English well, but do not try it, he will act as though he cannot. When someone addressed him he looked steadily at his interpreter. His eyes would flick back to the speaker only if he or she went on too long. One did not often witness such gracelessness in a head of state.

But of course, I thought, smiling over my cup of punch, he didn't have to worry about reelection, did he? There was no one here to make this joke to. I shared few jokes with the rest of Ivan's staff, which used to frustrate me, but I understood now that humor is one of the true cultural gaps, not easily bridged by mere linguistic proficiency, or even nearly four years' residence, as in my case. I rarely laughed at what I knew were considered perfectly respectable jokes by Ivan's cabinet, and similarly, whenever I said something quietly witty, I no longer expected acknowledgment of any kind. The source of the humor had to be extremely simple—a belch in a meeting, two whores in stilettos tripping on the sidewalk—for these men and I to have anything like a common response.

Dignitaries and the like approached Saeed one by one for more formal greetings; I would wait until the crowd had thinned, see if I could tease a bit more out of the interaction. So I stood in the corner chatting with Dr. Martinez, leader of one of the public health initiatives, to whom I often turned in these settings because he could be relied on to speak about only two subjects and with such enthusiasm that responses were hardly required: the health initiative and his very intelligent children. Then, one of the aides nodding to me, I crossed the room to meet Citizen Saeed.

I had expected Saeed might be displeased or confused by my appearance, but he did not seem to be in the business of having reactions. I presented him with a copy of my book, which he looked over for only a second before handing it to his aide, who placed it on a table among a range of gifts—local handicrafts, academic monographs on collective governance, biographies of the early revolutionaries.

He said something to his interpreter, who said: It is an American book.

I was born in Montana, I said, looking at him directly, though he looked only at the interpreter.

My research is an indictment of the Americans for their covert involvement in the last two coup attempts perpetrated against Ivan, I said, and waited.

Watching the interpreter Saeed raised his eyebrows in what may or may not have been comprehension, even affirmation, then shook my hand again by clasping it in both of his own. I wished to know whether this was a gesture all women received, and hoped I'd remember to ask someone later.

But even as I am somewhere momentous—the long-imagined home of my ancestors, the presence of a man who could only be called infamous—I am somewhere else. This has always been my weakness. At just the wrong instant, when I might have said something more, I had paused in thought, and was shuffled away, opportunity lost. I had been distracted by my desire to ask the foreign relations council if they had discussed with Saeed his recent suppression of his nation's indigenous pro-democracy movements, which I know had been of concern to Ivan, and in the US press was irrevocable confirmation of Saeed's iniquity. There was no way around it: the situation was distressing. No one could say what went on in Saeed's prisons. I might have said to him, *as a journalist with a profound commitment to human rights, I am deeply concerned...* Certainly opposition parties could never muster any presence within his borders; the regular sweeps kept everyone's heads down, even the pro-Western businessmen, who could make their money but had to watch their mouths like everyone else. There was no point in even bringing up the treatment of the Jews, not in this climate. Even Ivan would not have ventured to, though religious tolerance was one of his central reforms (another thing that distinguished him from the Americans thirsting for his blood, it should be noted). And what could I have said that would have been appropriate or had any effect? In some impulsive confrontation I might have surprised myself and even Ivan, but Saeed?

When Saeed dismissed me I got another drink, hoping he would notice, abstemious as he famously was. As far as I could tell he said nothing worthwhile to anyone. His handclasp had been very gentle, though whether this was intentional or simply indolence I didn't know. I had met no one remotely similar to compare him to, and couldn't say if my disappointment in the evening, the dullness that had suffused the event, was of note or also to be expected.

I lingered late in my office, skimming Human Rights Watch reports about Saeed's last year of governance. It was after midnight and the punch hadn't worn off, had left me jittery alone in the darkened wing. The photograph of my grandmother lay in my lap, though I did not remember why I'd taken it out, and didn't need to look down at the girl in it—gangly, holding hands with a sister who had died in her fourth childbirth, so I had been told—to know that it was only and subtly about the mouth that I resembled her.

There was a knock at my door; to my surprise it was Ivan. I knew that he often read late at night in his rooms, but I didn't usually see him, not in the hallways or elevator and certainly not on the lower stories.

I forgot I had something for you, he said. From a pocket in his suit jacket he retrieved an envelope.

Through the white paper I saw clouds of deep pink: three of the entrail-like flowers, dried and pressed, an acrid note to their odor.

I didn't know if you had seen them, he said. You should mail them to your grandmother in Montana, I promise you she will be delighted to see them.

Thank you, I said.

I kissed him on the cheek. One or both of us smelled of alcohol.

That is very kind, I said. He was smiling and stepping back, his hand on the doorknob.

How do you think the visit went? I said.

The visit?

Citizen Saeed's visit.

Ah, he said, funny—most of the time I forget you are a foreigner, but sometimes your words, they betray you. Visits are for little things, you know, if I stop by your house and we drink something together, or even tonight, if I come by your office, that is a visit. For matters of government we would not use this word.

I'm sorry, I said, I guess I'm still learning, and I laughed, unnecessarily.

You had a chance to speak with him, did you not?

Yes, I said. But it is, you know, it is an impossible situation.

Ivan nodded, looking toward the window, where the siren lights from the street flashed through the gaps in my blinds. Yes, that is a good way to put it. Or perhaps it is not impossible enough.

Before I could reply, Ivan said: Now what inspired your grandmother to leave such a beautiful village?

My grandfather, I said. He was an American.

He came here for business?

Research, I said, he was an anthropologist.

Ah yes—Ivan smiled—of course. An intelligent, curious man, a beautiful girl. Well, she will be very pleased to hear of your visit—and he waved his hand at the envelope I now held—Good night.

My grandmother is dead, I should have said.

How absurd that would sound. I hoped I had thanked him sufficiently. The flowers were delicate and several petals had already detached. I put the envelope in my desk drawer, where I would see it often.

# ALICE

Out my window there's only city and haze. No one I meet speaks of the sea. At night in my room the air conditioner is a whistling breath, an old man sucking in through his nose.

In bed I imagine myself on another coast, across the country, my back warm in sand and stone on a peninsula, sea to the east, bay to the west. Years ago I went to this place. The bay was quiet, waves high as a small dog, and not far from me two heavy women reprimanded a toddler that must have been the offspring of one. The trees were small, winter wind kept everything sparse. Not far from the beach—the sign for the turnoff just up the road—one could tour the remains of a Civil War prison, built on the sea for security and housing tens of thousands of Confederate POWs through the course of the war.

It's been years but I can picture it. In a nearby inlet a reconstructed colonial ship marks the place in the harbor where Europeans first set foot. The ship is dainty, fine for the flat pond of the bay, but what about the months crossing? What a heaven this place must have seemed, look around at the green shores, the bay water golden with afternoon, fish plentiful in the light. Up the hill a colonial town, briny air and roses trained around trellises, trellises encircling a fountain, further on a few colonial buildings kept up with unflagging authenticity, placards detailing all.

In my mind this is the shore I'm upon, the sand I stretch out in. The low trees cast a scattered shade, which I shuffle toward as the sun travels and skin heats up. A lighthouse towers somewhere behind me. Now I lie naked upon the shore, mothers' voices grown distant, far from me any thought of prison ruins, or the recurring image: in its revolutions the beam of the lighthouse illuminating my form. I am nothing, this peninsula a finger beckoning the sea toward the bay, the bay extending miles, on the horizon evergreen and rock in a code that discloses the distant shore and its islands. I close my eyes and I am inundated. Or my body extends and I touch both bodies of water, bridge the peninsula with the long yards of my spine. I run a hand over my hip, the air conditioner whistles keenly. I turn over, and upon the shore with me now, against my will, is Modigliani. Which ends every fantasy, every imagined rock I'd pressed a cheek to, the smell of kelp in the heat on the sand, all the nameless birds. I can't ask him to go because I know what he'll say, and say it mildly, not offended, not anything. And who am I to dissent, I who would abandon wherever I may be, this room, its damaged blinds, light striped across the sheets and me within them. Modigliani's hand is under my neck, pressing the base of my skull. I will myself to sink back into dream, but the shore is gone.

# SAM

*T*he day they found Shahid's body I wasn't writing, not a word. I was babysitting, drinking too much tea and fielding unending questions about homework. My sister-in-law had needed to cross the city to see a doctor about her pregnancy. Bleeding, my wife had said, which her sister would not have disclosed. You can type, answer your phone, all that at their home, my wife had said. Usually I adored how her remnant unease with the language made her say things like *type* when she meant *write*, but today I was irritated, I who had worked so hard but unsuccessfully to rid myself in every dialect of an American accent.

When the phone call had come from Shahid's editor, his own Italian accent so strong I had to ask him to repeat and repeat again, I cried out. The children must have looked up, seen me standing, my head against the door frame and the door open, I had meant to walk into the garden for better reception, but on hearing the news I was shrill as a hawk shrieking into a field. Afterward I was surprised both at the force of my reaction and the fact that the editor had called me at all, a choice I couldn't quite justify. The police called you? I asked the Italian, who said no, it was only that he had been phoning Shahid at the very moment they pulled his body from the canal, and someone had answered. If he was in the canal, I said, how did his phone still work? I don't know, the Italian said. But I remembered: Shahid kept his phone zipped up in a waterproof sleeve, I am tired of getting new ones, he'd said, I spill tea all over myself at least once a month.

Shahid did not drown; he was beaten to death.

The canal was far enough from the city, a full hundred kilometers, that they might have thought he wouldn't be found.

But no—how then would his death have served as warning? Without a body the message, as they say, could not be received. They'd dumped him, checked the lock schedule, and known that before long his name would turn up in the news.

Once the Italian hung up I sat down in the garden with a cold tea and was still there when Fawzia returned from her appointment, her expression concerned as she came through the gate, or perhaps it was merely the fatigue of the bus ride. When she saw me her face changed in a way I couldn't describe, and I realized from her sharp question that she feared something had happened to her sister, my wife. No, no, I said, seeing the children now gathered to the door, no, a friend, a friend is dead.

But I blame myself for using this word—was he a friend? We would chat, sometimes among others we would have a meal, but Shahid was not what you'd call friendly, and though you'd nudge him to tell a story or watch him as a joke was told, he maintained his charming but—I said to others and even once to him—overplayed reserve. In his absence we discussed how his sources among the insurgents were almost too good, his coverage of them almost too intimate. This isn't quite what we meant; rather, how in him pragmatism and zealotry were so potently allied. Will you come on for a segment about the murdered journalist? I got a call from the West Coast indie radio show I appeared on occasionally, and it was then that I skimmed the American press and saw Shahid's death had been noted even there—briefly, but noted. Of course, I said, he was a friend, and again I hadn't intended to use that word. *Colleague* would have been accurate, though *comrade* was what next occurred to me, despite its connotations, which were not what I meant and which would never have amused Shahid.

It seemed geography and profession had claimed us for the same side of whatever this was. For seven, eight years now US drones have bombarded the militant camps in the mountains, though protests grow more vehement and diplomatic relations more strained every year. Bombs land again on an impoverished village, or, in the brutal error the American military is almost laughably prone to, a wedding party. A boy escaping one strike runs up a mountain to be killed an hour later in another. Discovered among the dead in a camp of militants are a few members of the intelligence services. Allies, these nations, and yet. This spring the Americans dived out of the sky into an unassuming compound in the north, there to kill not any mere terrorist but the Director. Triumphantly they shot him in his bedroom, his children waiting on the balcony just outside. His body was thrown to the sea between the two nations. It was said he had lived here, allegedly undetected, for years. Such events can only remind one of the magnitude of their surveillance, my native country overseeing my present home, so that in moments of real emotion—vision misting in the garden, the Italian incomprehensible on the phone—I find myself subject to a humiliating self-consciousness, I look skyward and think I ought to go in. It's said that they located the Director by the vibrations of his windows, which when surveyed by laser over time confirmed that there was one more man conversing within the building than ever came out. Soon enough he was dead.

And so, the story somehow continues, was Shahid.

Shahid who didn't even trust waiters, met his sources amid the crowd on a bus or the thick of a market.

We should talk, I said to him, after he'd congratulated me on a piece in which I'd nearly proved that the intelligence services had interfered in a local election to the southeast, prevented a recount that had wide popular support. He looked more interested than I expected. Yes, let's meet next week, he said, his eyes bright through dirty glasses. But time passes and six weeks later he was dead.


What could I say to the radio show, to the US press, to anyone? Shahid, I might begin, had shown great courage and had remarkable access to both military and insurgent sources. Which is how he could so condemningly detail the degree to which the former had been infiltrated by the latter. How often the military seemed in its so-called victories in the mountains to leave supply lines open; when they moved into villages somehow only a few token fighters remained. But just what could anyone prove? Few—really no one other than Shahid—ventured into that territory to see for themselves, since journalist after journalist had been kidnapped there.

A few months ago when the navy had quietly purged its ranks of suspected infiltrators, a vicious attack on one of its bases followed, thirteen dead. A base not far at all from a nuclear facility. This was the focus of Shahid's latest stories, as fervent as always and as always with his beautiful sources—sources to die for, the now appalling phrase we'd used. These sources claimed that the insurgent infiltration of the military's ranks was so profound that any attempt to resist would be cause for war, a war in which, given the speed and brutality of the retaliation, the thirteen dead sailors, it must be said that the insurgents were holding their own.

I could only recite Shahid's achievements, with perhaps a critical gloss, and offer a few trite sentences on the man himself. What his murder might mean for journalism in this besieged nation. We all wanted to write his story, to do it justice. But despite all intentions and accusations, fingers pointed even by American generals, the sentence endured, implacable: *The intelligence services deny any involvement in the journalist's death.*

I couldn't say how much Shahid's death might disturb the economies by which so many across factions survived. His sources among the militants would never talk to me—no one will talk to an American, the others assured me. We sat around at dinner again, late, very late, so that the heat had at last somewhat subsided, and insects gathered deafeningly to the lamps, cigarette after cigarette did not drive them off. It was the sort of gathering Shahid would rarely have attended and which since his death I had frequented. No one will talk to an American. But no one will torture and kill me, either, I said, then recalled that the facts did not back me up on this, and there was general laughter, though I wished for silence. Beyond the lamplight the sky was a deep haze and I was too drunk. Somewhere to the east a drone dipped into the mountains.

We went on with our work, the intelligence services

went on with theirs. A week later one of Shahid's sources turned up: killed in an American strike. He was high up in the chain, a prize for any reporter or soldier; his number, it was said, appeared every few days in Shahid's phone. Of the two he got the better death—gone in the explosion, not for him broken ribs, ruptured organs, the numbered lacerations we read of in the autopsy report on our colleague. Well, I'd written nothing of Shahid's murder, but at least—I might joke, on the right night, in the right company—at least my fellow countrymen had not been left empty-handed.

*Unmanned* is an interesting word, I said to my wife.

Why do you always use that word? she said.

It's correct, I said, it's what everyone says, the drones are—

No, she said, *interesting*, this is such an American word, to Americans everything is always *interesting*.

I was just making an observation, I said.

No, she said, I mean, yes, this is what I am saying, it's only *interesting* when it happens to someone else.

Unmanned, I said, smiling, I am unmanned!

She nodded, then shook her head. I as a woman am always unmanned, she said, and what does that mean?

But I didn't reply, thinking then of Shahid, whose habits—cell phone zipped up in its sheath, head near a stranger's on a bus—in death became facts, stagnant and singular. Picture the Director, shrouded and sinking into the waves. His enemies wouldn't permit him a body: a symbol the living could claim.

*To claim a body*, I said aloud once my wife had left,

144

and I ran my fingers over the keyboard. Those who'd whis-pered their truths and half-truths to Shahid may now be silent, their souls still burdened. I would hear you, I said, but my words meant nothing to the night, through the smog the winking stars.

**M**odigliani came over, a bottle brown-bagged in his hand. I'd hoped for wine but it was gin. He poured for us both and produced a jar of olives from his jacket, with his fingers dropped three into each glass. Thank you, I'm sure, I said, eyeing the greasy floating pimentos. Your table sucks, he said, rocking it back and forth with his hand.

The death of Farzad Ahmad Muhammad, I said.

OK, Modigliani said.

You remember it, I insisted. He was murdered in US custody. A British journalist got interested, and so there was an actual military follow-up. A few guys were held responsible, or kind of—I pushed photos toward him, tapped each face in turn—this one spent two months in jail, this one was demoted, this one not even discharged. These photos, I added, were Kareem's. He was working on some kind of amateur investigation.

OK, Modigliani said.

Modigliani bent down and slid the lid of the olive jar under the short leg of the table. Now we have to finish these, he said. How did he die?

I said: He was hanging from the ceiling by his hands, which is common practice, but he was left there for days, and they beat his legs to interrogate him, the backs of his knees. *Pulpified*, is how the autopsy describes his legs—if he hadn't died, they'd have had to amputate. They said the beatings were normal, but none of them realized how many teams were going at him, how many altogether, and blood pooled around the injuries until his heart stopped, with him just hanging there. They found him on the morning of the fifth day.

Modigliani nodded. And where does Kareem come in?

He knew one of the guys who was later held responsible, the guy who went to jail. They were based out of the same compound for a while, they met socially, if that's the right word. I'm trying to see if maybe Kareem is the one who tipped off the journalist in the first place. Like, he gathered this evidence to give it to her.

And this works out to a motive for killing Kareem, what, seven or eight years later?

Fuck, I said, fuck.

Modigliani stacked the photos and pushed them back toward me, maneuvering around drinks and olives. He said: If the guy who killed the prisoner was Kareem's friend, Kareem could have been looking to get him off, not get him punished. But you know that. Not to mention, he added, that we have four other victims.

I know, I said. The photo on top was of the bruised legs, and I covered it with both hands.

Alice—Modigliani said, looking in the direction of the air conditioner—your thinking is the opposite of conspiratorial. It's the web without the spider.

He said: I think I've always liked that about you.

Later I understood this was the one thing he ever said that I truly believed.

If I were a conspiracy theorist, he went on, I'd think you were trying to distract this investigation from its real target.

Bill LeRoy, I said obediently, Xenith.

Right now he's angling to replace the military in Afghanistan, Modigliani said. All private contractors, private air force. British East India Company model.

I said: At the same time he's selling his forces to countries hoping to keep migrants in or migrants out. Or rather, Muslims out. Turn back the boats at gunpoint.

Modigliani shifted and I thought he was going to lay his hands over the photo, over my own.

What happens, I wondered, when a spider mistakes itself for a fly?

Modigliani finished his drink and rose. The table rocked again.

Have you ever noticed, he said, how rarely I ask a question?


After Modigliani left I went on: I'd called the guy who'd served time, the guy Kareem knew. He was punished most severely because he'd visited the prisoner the most and was supposed to be the one signing off, keeping track of the others.

I was only halfway through Kareem's name when the woman who had answered the phone interrupted: He doesn't know anything. Don't call here again. She was gone and with her the background sound of a child's off-key singing. I called again. I thought of going out there, to the Midwestern farmland where they lived, not far from where I used to visit a long-dead uncle of my mother's. Amish in buggies or on bicycles on the road's shoulder, cornfields, trampolines in yards that back then I'd coveted. He was a farm boy, this man, and at first I thought this should damn him. Shouldn't a boy like that have known, have understood the body and what it won't endure? Only once did they unhook Muhammad from the ceiling and by then he could no longer bend his knees. But tonight, the refrigerator assuming the role of crickets, the floor athrum with someone's bass, I understood why this made no difference.

Just last week I received in the mail a copy of my old chapter on Anastasia Calque, with one of my best lines (I had thought at the time) double underlined:

Each story is the story of a marriage, and who is dead in the end.

Well, I had written it; I would write nothing like it now, but what does that matter? I am no longer young and no longer need to mean everything always, like some sort of monk or machine.

My work on Calque and her minor novel *Eyes of the Moth* is still widely cited. The novel had vanished, out of print, long before Calque's death, her death which must now be, it is strange to think, thirty years ago. She had died without heir and her effects were left neglected in her apartment, which a trollish distant cousin or aunt now inhabited. After a decade of unanswered letters, one of Anastasia's former lovers had in frustration shown up at the door, to plead with the aunt for one afternoon to sort and catalog Anastasia's things. There must be letters from her godfather, the lover had persuaded the aunt, and these will be worth something. The godfather was long dead, but his films were now being remastered, and had there been anything more than a few snapshots of him, in his silly signature high-waisted pants, eating ices with the young Calque on a dock, seagulls wheeling, no doubt they would indeed have sold. It was then that the lover had discovered Calque's neat boxes of original manuscripts, among them *Eyes of the Moth*, which she retrieved, the aunt's acquiescence reluctant. Thus seventeen years ago a copy of the novel had appeared in my department mail. Courtesy of this same former lover, whose note to me, in English, said only: *This must be published. E.*

At that time, of Calque's five novels only one had been translated into English—by, it's worth noting, the new husband of this same E, Calque's erstwhile lover. The rest of Calque's work was read ravenously and to some degree canonized in her home country, but never known or wholly forgotten outside it. The rest except for *Eyes of the Moth*, that is, which had never been available anywhere after the first print run was lost to fire. A handful of copies had always been said to have survived the flames, and in the years before E's package arrived I had attempted several times to obtain one, although at least twice I'd paid through the nose for what turned out to be the wrong book—refunds of course, in the unhinged capitalism of that country, impossible.

The fire had been no accident; rather a deliberate attack on the house that published all the great leftist writers of the time. It was the eve of the military coup, and it was never at least to my research definitively clear which of the pathetic right-wing or neo-fascist gangs then roaming the streets, their moment imminent, was responsible. A custodian, a mail clerk, and a young editorial assistant had died. Quite the offensive on the intelligentsia. The other victims, however, were the novels in the print shop, still in the midst of being bound, and this included

Calque's newest, a fictionalization of her love affairs, all the participants perfectly recognizable, though portrayed in grotesque and radiant distortion. This trueness to life, as well as the novel's radical sexual politics, would no doubt have won it considerable if not positive attention. But only six weeks after the fire came the coup, and nationwide there was little attention left for literature. By the time anyone could have tried to salvage the lost novels, the military junta was in its furious first round of censorship and reforms, and Calque had withdrawn in illness to her apartment, in the first stages of the malaise that would find her years later immensely and debilitatingly fat.

I do not deceive myself. I know the novel is flawed, knew it the first time I read it, at my desk turning the pages with care and sitting very upright. Calque's work is so sickeningly violent, and yet I succumb, each time it offers up a sentimental morsel, too sweet, I know, but swallow anyway, and in the throat it is monstrous, a moth with razor-edged wings. It is never wise to read her fiction quite alone, as I did then, around me the building a series of settling and humming sounds, growing louder as the novel's lovers destroyed one another, with grisly intimacy, as if the tongue could lift skin clean off bone. Perhaps it was in this vulnerable state—sitting in my office, teaching too much in those days and still alone in the city, my fingers crept to the lap of my skirt as I read, Calque's lovers encountering one another in cinemas (of course), in baths, and by the light of an aquarium—that I fell in love with the novel. Despite its flaws. Despite or because of. As they say. But I have reread it at least a dozen times.

I wrote the introduction to the translation, which

came out a few years later, and my paper on Calque's oeuvre, which focused on this novel as stylistic keystone, the last to be written before her psychiatric treatments commenced, had been lauded, contended with, and was if not essential certainly a significant contribution to my vita when I was named chair. Calque is not of course the primary focus of my research; rather the poetry of that time, in the publishing wasteland left in the wake of the coup, no one able or desiring to publish under the censorship of the military regime, and so appearing in journals and underground publications across the continent, engaging in a bewitchingly fertile series of translations and collaborations with foreign artists in an effort to resist the cultural ruination taking place in their homeland. With her French name and French father Calque could have fled for Paris, but she did not. By that time she was too ill. And, she claimed, she hated Paris.

She claimed she hated everywhere that was not her apartment. *Where I was a girl*, she said in interviews, *hiding in the cupboards with my cousin during dinner parties, listening to every small thing that went on.* Consider how debauched her mother's parties were. Shortly after he reached puberty the cousin became quite volatile, his psychiatric problems ultimately not unlike Calque's, but he was a boy, and big, and when he broke the arm of a teacher in one of his spells, he was sent to his first institution, and died some fifty years later in his fourth. And so Calque spent the junta years in her apartment, writing little, and occasionally, when illness overtook her, traveling to a northern hospital to convalesce, a luxury not widely available under the new regime, but with her mother's money she could seek out what vestiges remained.

Calque did not travel well, as I had explained in my papers, and my central illustration of this fact and of her instability in those days was the story of the photographer. She had stayed with the photographer in America only a few months, and yet what a wreck she'd been on returning, her symptoms heightening so that she would never again go abroad; and this could fairly be said to be the only time in her forty-nine years that she turned to drink.

My most thorough treatment of the photographer was in the chapter on Calque in my book on the art of the junta years, a chapter developed and adapted from my many previous critical writings on her life and work. By my reading, the writer's disastrous relationship with the photographer paralleled the relationship between their two nations. She: under siege, desperate, celebrated artist on the verge of exile, fighting for her work's existence. He: in the nascence of his talents, wealthy, hardly knowing his own power, recent tribulations overcome and his success merely in its first flowering. Calque had seen some of his work and after an ardent correspondence had traveled to New York to see him. Her first novel had met with some success, despite its controversial subject and the increasingly grim state of her country; she was high with her new status, if not manic. She packed up and flew to him.

*Each marriage is the story of a marriage*
*Whose is the end*


And now, after years of dormancy, the story resumes: last week the photographer wrote to me. My book has been out almost a decade, but here was my chapter on Calque,

Xeroxed and mailed back to me, with his enraged cover letter and that line crudely emphasized. I am not dead, the photographer wrote, you may be dismayed to learn. And all you have written about me are lies.

He must be in his eighties now, but he was quite articulate, his penmanship picturesque. The English translation of the novel in which he appeared, the same *Eyes of the Moth*, had come out twelve years earlier, a few years before my own book. Yet it seemed these events had escaped his notice until now, when they left him belatedly apoplectic—dangerously so, I thought, considering his age, and impressed that even as his insults mounted his handwriting did not waver. It was interesting that more of her lovers had not protested her treatment of them, whether in life or literature; the E who had sought out her manuscripts was the only one as far as I knew whom she had not pinned down in a novel somewhere. (Though I've wondered if this kindness was strategic, since E's new husband had proved himself such an adept translator.)

Pure libel, the photographer wrote, and demanded immediate redress. His first example was that I had explained—as Calque said many times through the years—that on her arrival in New York he had refused to take her picture because she was too fat. This, she said in interviews, in her murmuring voice and with her cat-like expression, this broke my heart. He would only photograph my ankles, she said, which are still very beautiful.

Soon, she said, he only photographed women with ankles like mine. If you look closely, she said, you'll see the likeness, all the ankles are mine.

Utter nonsense, the photographer wrote. Though I, who had pored over what slides of his work I could find (he had not, in fact, become the success his early shows had promised; after the reviews cooled then ceased altogether, he had turned to advertising and spent much of his career working for a mid-range watch company), believed I could see just what she meant.

Dear sir, I began in reply. Thank you for your letter. The novel has two sides; I would say it is two mirrors back to back. Any I is split from the start: two faces made one, the stone and the acid that bleeds it. I have forgotten your work, but I do remember Calque's ankles, perfect half-moons, expensive shoes resting on the platforms of her wheelchair. We shook hands.

In the novel the photographer is less than a beast: one-dimensional. Every day the woman flees him; he closes the door to his studio and she takes a train into the city, where she seeks out a neighborhood known for its radicals as well as its junkies, all day she sits in a dark room and hears a chorus of laughter and vomit and copulation, a woman tirelessly serenading herself. An old man befriends her, amateur gnostic, long-time addict. With him she pretends to pray. Though insincerely, merely to quiet his fears for her.

The photographer is passionate about Eastern thought and eats one meal a day, always in some sort of broth. She hides all her chocolate, which he is sick even to look at. The day she leaves him there is an ice storm, ice sheathing every twig of the oaks on the boulevard that leads to his house, ice on the tracks shutting down the trains that run from the suburbs into the city, ice snapping whole limbs to litter roads and smash porches and roofs. She is caught in a police sweep of the building she passes her days in, but everyone else, it seems, had been warned; she is the only one there. After her release she flies home. Her clothes are stained with chocolate and she has grown only fatter.

Why must I write what you've already read? When he loses her the photographer believes he has known suffering, but he is mistaken. I do not know if he ever marries.


Calque was nowhere near radical enough for her fellow intellectuals under the right-wing regime. In time they condemned her, expelled her from their journals, their collaborations, their salons. She wrote only of sex and children and God. When I met her she asked me, You didn't bring your daughter? I said, No. I said, I hadn't realized I'd told you about her. (Louisa was so young then, just two, and the research trip on which I met Calque my first time away from her.) Of course I could tell from your voice, Anastasia said, on the phone you have the voice of a mother. She laughed, and her nurse, with whom she had no languages in common, laughed with her.

Calque never had children and by then her husband was dead.

Years later she drowned, a seemingly accidental result of her medications and an oversized bathtub.


I wrote my letter to the photographer in the margins of the novel, on only the pages in which he appears. Not the translation, but the original: one of the rare extant copies, which I had through years of diligence at last acquired.

It was a gift, then, of some value, or would have been had I not defaced it. He had never learned her language, of course. Calque was—all agreed—a linguistic genius, and learned English as though it were an extended joke, punchline delayed; she claimed she learned only from television programs, but her vocabulary was multifarious and syntax dizzying. To this I myself can attest. She knew when she wrote the story of the photographer that he couldn't read it; it was only upon the translation of *Eyes of the Moth*, after her death, and with my own writing about her that he could learn the role she'd assigned him. He told me Anastasia had read him everything she'd written, in her own flawless translations, as they sat on the porch among the fireflies and lush green of Westchester County. I did not believe him.

# ALICE

Someone might have said: Move on. Eight months since I'd entered those bloodied rooms, and what? At night I envisioned masked men flitting across the rooftop out my window, visible in the light not of the moon but this city's merciless incandescence. Who were these men, barely seen, passing through a mirror of my own mind? In my dreams in what guise did the killers appear? Mercenary, militant, operative, terrorist, troop, fool... Whose face turned away from me? Who got rich in the end? I stood before the window, bare belly to the air conditioner, in one hand a glass of warm gin.

Around me the apartment was like a home—Kareem's investigation pinned up in one corner, a folding table I'd found in a dumpster and hauled up the stairs bearing my notes, my clothes folded on the bookcase, beside the bed a stack of magazines. The old smell was gone, my smell must have driven it out. Whatever admixture of raisin bran, gin and lime, Corona and lime, perfume, and purple dish soap defined me.

Home to what? For what? I'd written three pieces on the whole mess, and someday I would write, I might write, something on Xenith. Not tonight and not tomorrow. I wasn't broke. I was working on a story on the high accident rates among veterans, everything that could not be called suicide but betrayed exceptional recklessness. I pressed my forehead against the window, butt thrust out to keep my skin's distance from the chill air.

After the hurricane shootings—after I had left the city, left it all unsolved—I had gone up to some little college city where a series of fights and two rapes had occurred that seemed to be racially motivated. The city was Victorian coal-era rowhouses, nice shabby brick or quaintly painted facades. Half the college's buildings were on the historical register. I did my best. Some said that this was in fact my best piece. Most cohesive, this was the phrase, though who would have read enough of my work, the whole corpus, if you will, to compare? My disdain for the place swelled up in every preposition, I couldn't comprehend why I was there, tripping over Adirondack chairs and trying to charm these baby-faced brutes, when the hurricane shootings remained unavenged.

But that can't be the right way to remember it. That can't be right. I was the one who had decided to leave the hurricane behind me, forget whoever we'd found in the morgue. Forget all the ways there now were to raise a gun, to deny an insurance claim, to buy or sell someone else's land. I'd had a beautiful grant, I could have lived off the hurricane for years. I wasn't broke. I was tired of wearing the same T-shirts, everything I owned stank of a perversion of perfume, sweat, sewage, the dead. Was I just tired? The feds dawdled and that city sat in its stink and tears. The militias were gathering, we could all sense their presence, two bodies—our two bodies, Modigliani and I claimed them, a man and woman we'd never known—should have sufficed as evidence, and yet we had nothing. Modigliani and I, nothing. Every night it was as if we had to stand before the figurative chalkboard and rub away the script in which we'd written each name, each suspicion, and the trace of those failed phonemes endured on the side of my fist. And now it seemed clear that had I found 2,000 more perfect words, something or everything might have been different, or at least I might have been. As for the dead, what could be done for them, though they cry out for justice—a phrase I hope I would never write.

The PTSD doctor at the VA hospital had grown unexpectedly fond of me, and once was I believe on the verge of asking me over to dinner. With no grounds I suspected Modigliani had said something to her. But what did he ever say? Lately I wondered if he was even in this city anymore, or if he left for the better part of each week, I even tailed him once to the airport, sure the whole time that he knew I was there.

It's my sense of time that fails me: never exploiting myself, or not soon enough, as a body within it. Your timing's just off, an editor had said to me once and convincingly. So I had wandered away from the hurricane, and now I was again paralyzed, looking out over this, the original corrupt city, where I hadn't found even one bar I could sincerely enjoy. I blew on the window as though to fog it, write with a fingertip. There was a knock at the door.

Was I a fool to hope as I crossed the room? It was some sort of workman. Did you call about a fridge? he said. I was wearing only a bra and jeans with the belt undone. Not me, I said, not smiling, and closed the door.

When I turned around the room was as it always was. In that college town I had taken to going to an open mic every week at this coffeeshop, a bunch of townies strumming guitars or reading wretched poetry. One woman performed famous monologues. I had an idea that this experience was amusing, authentic, or better than being alone.

One man, a devotee of Cat Stevens, gave me his number, and a few days later I called it, didn't leave a message, and didn't pick up the five times he called back. When he wrote the number on the side of my disposable cup, gripping it doggedly, I knew this was more or less what would happen. I made a deal with myself that I would go until the woman got to the opening of *Richard III*. As it turned out she never did, not in my time there. To the south that city still sang its long dirge, its people scattered, and among the thousands a man and a woman lay dead, victims of some human crime, murdered, the mythic time of the storm like a map lost in the waves. I think this now, I don't know what I thought then.

That is correct. I was not in the room.

We were stationed in the hallway and tasked with preventing any interference with the execution of the sentence.

Yes, I mean the execution, the sentence was an execution. That's what I meant.

Yes, ma'am, and to ensure that the body was properly handled.

I'm not personally familiar with the burial customs.

There were several employees of the state morgue, as well as a religious official of some kind responsible for that.

All I meant was, we were there to ensure that the body was properly secured and transported to the proper location. That nobody photographed it or stole it or whatever.

That is correct.

We learned about the video the same way you all did, on the internet. I heard about it from—

Ma'am, we had no orders to search the staff, so I don't know how we could have prevented it. It's a local problem.

I don't need to speak the language to search someone for a camera phone.

No, that's correct.

And I do appreciate your point. I just don't think—

We were outside in the hallway, like I stated. You can actually see the hallway in the video. Before the stairs to the gallows, which just looks like a big platform.

The guy with the camera would have been standing at the bottom of the stairs, you can tell from the angle.

There were no Americans in the room. We were stationed outside, in the hallway. We were under orders not to go into the room or participate in any way.

That's correct. No Americans, no women.

Well, you can see in the video that they were all wearing masks, and everybody I saw go into the room was wearing a mask, but I can't guarantee anything, seeing as there could have been some men already in the room before I was stationed outside. Or any of them could have removed their masks when they got in the room, obviously.

It was his request to leave his face uncovered. He was definitely offered the hood.

Not by me personally. I did not interact with the prisoner.

There were thousands of hangings under his regime, a lot of them in that room, as I understand.

I'm not an expert. I believe so.

I can't speak to that.

When I first saw the video, I thought maybe it was his idea.

To get his supporters outraged. So you can see his face.

That's an advantage in terms of the video, but it was in no way necessary, there were doctors on hand to certify it was him, using fingerprints and other means. I personally saw him enter the room and saw his body exit it.

Stranger things have happened.

I'm not sure what they're saying. He says something back, you can see his lips move.

From where I was I couldn't hear.

I heard the shouting, absolutely. But as I said, we were under orders not to go in.

I thought I heard the crash when the trapdoor opens, like you hear it in the video, but I can't say for sure.

One thing was the name of the insurgent leader, the cleric. His father was also a rebel. The father was executed back in the '90s and now the son runs half the city. He's our real problem now.

That's one way to look at it.

I'm not familiar with the customs. I heard he's buried with his sons, in the same graveyard, which if you ask me seems like a pretty good deal.

The doctor was already in the room. Then the body was removed by a professional team, which we let in.

That is absolute rumor and speculation.

I've seen the photo. But maybe the rope did that, injured his neck like that. I'm not a forensic expert. I personally supervised the removal of the body and there was no interference of any kind whatsoever.

You think someone could have stabbed him a whole bunch of times without us noticing?

There wasn't even any time. If it did happen, which in my opinion it absolutely did not, it happened off-site, when the body was in local custody.

That was not our responsibility.

Someone would have had to have a knife obviously, to cut the rope.

I can't speak to that.

He was in a body bag when he passed us, it was unzipped just enough so we could get a visual ID.

I can attest that we were all doing our due diligence.

No, that is correct.

It was not our responsibility to—

I don't see how he could have been stabbed while he was alive because you see him die in the video. And don't tell me that fall didn't kill him. Either way there would have been blood in the room, and we saw no evidence—

In my personal and professional opinion.

It appears to be a stabbing wound, sure, but it's just a photo and can be altered or whatever.

I don't know anything about that. But he definitely would have been dead by then.

You said desecrated, ma'am, those were not my words. And the thing is, even if he deserved it, I agree—

You have no idea who these guys are working for, they could have been working for him and five other guys, you don't know. That's how things are done there. It's like, some of them are working for us and for the terrorists, every week, two paychecks. You have no idea, I mean listen to all the stuff people were shouting in there. I hope for the sake of law and order and the sort of peace of the country that nothing happened, but for him, it's like, what can you expect. But nothing did happen, as I said, and if any of it happened, it was after he was already dead.

I think you're missing the point, ma'am, is all.

Like I said, not under my immediate supervision.

Right. None of us saw anything with our own eyes.

*I* discovered Diana's fake name, and why did it take me so long? Artemis. I looked up at my rearview as though her spirit might be at a steering wheel in pursuit in the night. The rehab facility she'd gone to was on the exact other side of the country—fold a map in half and the two towns could have kissed.

A woman who had been there at the same time as Artemis had agreed to talk to me if we met far from her home, location her choice. Indeed the zoning here seemed to value anonymity above all, a late capitalist mode as bleak as the Soviet style it contested: everywhere strip malls, everywhere the same stores repeated, variety solely in the names of the pizza shops or occasional sign indicating the way to historical sites one was sure one had already seen. A lot of development around here, I said blandly to the man at the hotel front desk, and in his heavy accent he began to recount in detail the area's history, slow road to its current afterlife: how waterways had been the only streets, which was why there were no town centers and now only sprawl, and how in the last few decades the oystermen and tobacco farmers had been disappearing. Meaning not that the men themselves had perished, only their vocations fallen away.

I arrived at the meeting place, a hibachi steakhouse, and sat far from the windows, near the kitchen, as instructed. Despite its outdated signage and view onto a parking lot, inside the restaurant was bright and tranquil, except for the music, which lent even the flat planes of tofu a frenetic gleam. I had come early, and pulled out a notepad that the waitress glanced at as she poured my tea. Jean arrived twenty minutes before our appointed time.

Jean wasn't her name, but that's what she'd asked to be called.

She looked around as though the dining area were interesting, and after shaking my hand opened the menu to read it slowly, on each of her false nails a rhinestone, white, blue, green. She ordered a full meal, I a cucumber salad.

Did you know about Artemis's murder before I called? I asked.

She shook her head.

She was shot? she said. I nodded.

It's so sad, she said, I've been having nightmares.

Her soup arrived, and she said nothing until it was gone, when she resumed: She was really into guns, you know, she used to go do target practice. There's a gun range near the facility, though you wouldn't think there would be. I never went.

Did she consider herself in danger, I said, was there—

Everything's confidential, she said.

I understand, I said, I won't use your name.

No, no, I mean, everything's confidential that happens there. I don't think I can tell you what she said or what goes on in the meetings or anything. It's a sacred space.

And so it went and after half an hour I had nothing but the confirmation that the woman whose picture

I showed her had indeed been in treatment for the dates I'd already confirmed, and that this woman said she had a daughter, Jean had once seen a picture of her.

Mixed-race, she said.

So is my nephew, she added.

Did she talk about the girl's father?

Jean shook her head. I understood this to mean a refusal of the question and not a reply.

I don't know his name, she said, I'm sorry.

It's all right, I said, I do.

What is it? she said.

That hardly seems fair, I said.

I had shown her photos of the other four victims, expecting nothing, which is what she offered.

Most women are murdered by someone they know, usually a partner, she said.

I mean, most women who are murdered, she added.

But in this case there were the four others, I said. I leaned forward, a droplet of tea falling onto my thumbnail, and said: The police have no idea who did this. Anything you could tell us—

She nodded, opened her mouth, but then said nothing, instead fidgeting with her blouse, which was tighter over her breasts than she seemed to have expected.

What made you choose this place? I asked.

I'm part of a group that does protests at the naval base, she said.

I was embarrassed by my surprise.

Protesting what? I said.

High-frequency sonar, she said. Actually, it's all unnecessary sonar testing, but we're focusing on high frequency. It's deadly for the whales. And no one has any idea about the wider effect on ocean ecosystems. I got interested eight years ago when there was a test here—did you hear about it? I shook my head. Anyway, there was a sonar test, although they didn't admit that, but eighteen whales beached themselves, you know, swam out of the water onto the shore to die, all within two days, which never happens. They were bleeding from their ears and in their brains, the scientists said. It was horrible. So first they say it's a big mystery, but it turns out there was a huge sonar test that same day, and this is happening all over wherever there's sonar tests. Whales and dolphins beaching themselves after. And you know, even if they don't beach themselves, it can still kill them, because they use their hearing to eat, and they stop hunting because of the noise and may not start up again because it's terrified them or even left them deaf or insane, and they starve to death. We only know about the ones that beach, but most whales when they die, they just sink to the bottom of the ocean. So I joined up with this local group that protests and tries to get guidelines in place that will protect the whales. And once we were thinking of doing this anti-whaling campaign, and we used to talk about pamphleting this restaurant and some other places, because the Japanese have such bad whaling policies, and one guy thinks they serve dolphin meat here. But then we decided not to, it didn't seem right to single out Japanese people, how would that look, and the dolphin-meat guy didn't seem that reliable. But anyhow, I was curious about the place, and no one would ever think of me coming here, you know?

I work at a restaurant by the naval base myself, she added, waitress. You probably figured—and with this for the first time she smiled.

Figured what, sorry?

Well, I look like a waitress, don't I? Everyone always knows, I don't even have to tell people. Don't put that in your article, though.

I won't, I said.

It's funny about people you meet in places like that, she said. It's like you're supposed to feel some connection.

She didn't go on.

You could help us, I said, you could help us figure out what happened to her.

I don't think so, she said. I don't think it's right to say things after she's dead. I probably should have said that on the phone. But I was so shocked when you said she'd been shot I wasn't thinking.

I watched her unfold a slice of pickled ginger with her fork. The bell by the door dinged twice and a group of businessmen shook hands by the window.

Five veterans were killed, I said.

She didn't say anything, then said: Artemis is the one who, when a man sees her naked, she turns him into a deer and his own dogs eat him?

Yes, I said. I think so.

I thought that's what I remembered. I think she told me that. Goddess of the hunt, that's what she'd say, when people asked. Almost everyone asked.


There was nothing for me but to go home. It was Christmas. I arrived a few days earlier than I'd meant to, I'd planned to visit a friend on the way but canceled when I learned she'd just had a third baby. Everywhere it was too warm, the earth soft, grass green. I walked jacketless on trails that other years had been inches iced over, the reservoir was dark and open, ice just a mucosal film across the shallows. It was so quiet, the geese gone, and always before there had been the serenata of water releasing beneath ice, deep pops and creaks resonating.

Climate change, my father said, washing plastic bags in the sink, the kitchen was festooned with bags.

We discussed the news and I made a soup.

In the backyard fat squirrels stretched themselves from tree trunk to birdfeeder, one leg akimbo. All day squirrels ate the birdseed and if it didn't snow soon who knew how fat they'd get: we'd wake up to find them gruesome on the patio, popped open like so many overfed ticks.

At various gatherings people asked me about the investigation, people had heard about the murders. When there was nothing to report I would comment on the weather or not quite say how long I'd be in town.

I kept my phone on silent but checked it twice an hour.

On the day the war ended—all troops out of Iraq, except for the thousands on the bases or who'd become private contractors, except for the thousands dead—I texted Modigliani to tell him. Like I had a scoop, this was my joke.

No reply.

I took long walks, by the reservoirs but also downtown to the old mills and the canals, stagnant this season, shopping carts shining in the turbid water. Christmas lights shown from an occasional window, the rest vacant or boarded up.

I arrived at the local bar each day just before or just after the mailman. I had one beer and sat too long, though no one minded, and I think if I'd ordered a second the bartender, fortyish and sweetly disproportionate, skinny with big fake boobs, wouldn't have charged me. I could be wrong.

I should have said something to Modigliani about our five—this is how I thought of them, that they had one family in life, another in death, here we were—something to mark the occasion: the end of their war. But what? If he had an appropriate sentiment he didn't offer it. I laid their photos out on my bed; I put them away.

On Christmas day we visited my grandmother: still spry, widowed four years before. Pineapple upside-down cake sat already in squares on small plates when we arrived. How was it that over many decades her parents and her husband had each died the week of Christmas? She was always the first to mention this, which was in its way a relief. On the small fake tree crystal ornaments tinkled with any movement—the enthusiasm of her small dog, any step across the room toward the jar of mint chocolates—and this noise, a peculiar family hymn, had traveled with me from childhood till now. Within a few years all the veterans of World War II would, like my grandfather, be dead, their war passing from memory into myth.

Before his death he had collected and typed up his letters home, which spanned his time in training through a year in the European theater. Each child and grandchild had received a bound copy. I had begun reading mine, then seemed to have mislaid it in one of my many moves, though I liked to think I was someone who might have an enduring core of possessions. There was probably another copy in this house, if I wished to find it. Although, after all, the war had been only a few years of his life.

And other than a few reconnaissance photographs—an avid amateur, he'd thought up a new way to take photos from artillery observation planes, in the one I knew best Dresden still smoldered, spire of the devastated cathedral in the foreground, around it roofs and walls everywhere destroyed, definition softened by smoke and ash—as far as I could tell his role was of no consequence to history.

*I* was the one who looked after the dogs.

The dogs showed up like strays and lurked like strays, but two had plump bellies and one a shine that fur can only be brushed to. It was my suspicion that folks were saving on doggy daycare, leading their pups down to the encampment when they went off to work and maybe not bothering to pick them up again. Figuring that's the sort of people we were, we'd love what others scorned, fork over our wages to any open palm, feed any open mouth, sponge-bathe a stranger while singing songs of freedom.

I had arrived at the encampment on its third day. At that time I was out of temp work and couch-crashing in Queens, a borough I had previously admired from afar. I'm going to the protest, I told my host, my friend is how I used to think of her, and she said: You'll fit in there. She revised that to: I wish I could come, and she picked up a toy dump truck, metonym for her responsibilities as well as the reason couch-crashers weren't her thing now, not like back when, fresh out of college, we'd all been different people, according to memory. It's good for America, she said. But what is America good for? the part of me that was overly influenced by her seven-year-old asked, not aloud. We hugged and I left, my backpack hitting the crucifix that hung in my opinion too near the coat rack, and I considered apologizing for all the jokes I'd made about her being *my host*, body of Christ, bread of heaven. But I never knew what her kids would repeat to her, so I took refuge in silence.

I'd tried one such joke out on the security guard at the last office where I'd worked reception, and it had gone very quietly.

I was good at that job but they hadn't renewed me.

I had worn, I want to attest, inarguable lipstick.

Every time someone asked me what brought me to the protest I said something different and true.

I love men in uniform, I said, and exhibited the welts from the last round of plastic handcuffs.

I love men in suits, I declared while pointing behind whichever journalist or civically minded tourist questioned me toward the few bankers who through arrogance or miscalculation walked right by our camp, in a sort of crisp scurry, not looking back at us in the manner of heroes on TV shows who know they're being followed, or alternatively looking with open disgust, their cell phones to their ears, as though this made their faces invisible. When they walk fast, I said, it really brings out the ass.

Later I said: I love the dogs.

Around me people made signs that I stood under or near.

I had good rapport with a girl who worked at a nearby corner store—we had both announced on meeting that the other looked just like someone she used to know, which was true on my part though I could not have said who, and I assume Alanza too (this was her name) was not lying. She let us use the bathroom and gave away merchandise that would have been chucked, well-aged plastic-wrapped muffins, that sort of thing, blistered hot dogs. The hot dogs were for the dogs. Due to their superior arts of persuasion Bighead and Beagle-mix ate the most.

A fellow protestor had taken to visiting me and the dogs a few times a day, with what I believed to be romantic intentions. Yet I admit that there was a great deal of kindness in that place, kindness I hadn't been fool enough to expect, so why should I introduce labels and through them the death of community?

What are their names? he asked, scratching the ears of the one whose ears everyone scratched, the Soft-Eared One.

They're not mine to name, I said.

I believe he liked this answer, and treated it as a sort of overture, in exchange for which (though should I not have critiqued this economy?) he offered me, next time, a book.

I brought you a book, he said.

I've read that, I said, which I had.

Crotchnose was offering his nose firmly and repeatedly to the crotch of a nearby Iraq War veteran, who shooed him off. When Crotchnose turned to the veteran's lady companion for consolation, I got a look like, why don't you do something?

I whistled, but it came out like a catcall. Sorry, I said, and tried again.

They don't even have collars, someone observed.

I had one hot dog saved up, hot dog beats crotch, and deployed it.

It took almost two weeks for the cops to start in about the dogs, but then it never ended, daily they said they'd call animal control. Fortunately the only thing I'd taught the dogs was to scatter when cops came, a trick that took little skill on my part, dogs by nature hate pepper spray.

By now between eight and ten were there all day every

day. In some quarters it was a cause for concern. I attended to every instance of defecation, which helped stave off complaints. Seemingly following the lead of Big-balls, the dogs agreed among themselves about peeing, almost never pissing on anything problematic. It is funny, I said to the veteran's companion, how they understand the difference between indoors and outdoors, as a concept beyond simply indoors and outdoors. They would never pee, for instance, on a tent or sleeping bag, or anywhere near the food.

The Beautiful Shining One was making the rounds, ambassador for the rest.

One night the veteran was speaking, we sat in a small circle, cold, Bookman having wrapped a blanket around my shoulders and the dogs making themselves useful by sleeping on feet, Bighead stretched thoughtfully over three pairs. The veteran paused and I said, My sister was in Iraq.

As a journalist, I added, gazing at the place in the circle where the campfire should be, now occupied by the Shining One.

The veteran said something appropriate but I was otherwise engaged, dissuading Crotchnose from some new arrivals. I don't know what else I would have said.

My host came to visit a few times and her eyes went big. Amazing, amazing, she said, touring the camp library, camp dining area, some meeting in progress, and discovering one of her old union reps to loudly embrace. Her boy was scared of dogs so I introduced him only to the Little One. My host had brought three casseroles and I told the boy that our task was to bring the casseroles to the pantry, so the whole camp could share them that night and the dogs lick the dishes. He walked beside me, glancing at Bighead, who stayed polite at my other side.

One day a banker brought two bags of dog food. From a paper bag he produced a stack of dog dishes and a jug of spring water.

This doesn't mean we're square, I said.

I'm actually an assistant, he said, I don't really work in finance.

I used to be a receptionist, I said, I didn't really work in just about everything.

We got to talking.

Every day the songs were more beautiful, and the speeches were shouted in unison line by line across the park so that lacking mike and amps the hundreds if not thousands could hear, and the speeches were more and more significant, at least that's what everyone said. Journalists gathered to us, filmmakers, old-time radicals, career activists, gender theorists, high-quality politicians, writers, actors, one by one they addressed the cameras and us. To stand in solidarity, they said. Not to stay, but to visit, I explained to Sweet Soft-eyes, who always sat at the front of the crowd.

Every week there were poetry readings and the poetry was really improving.

Bookman finally nailed it, bringing me a Gaddis I'd always meant to get to. Later I read him the highlights and he stroked the head of Old Baldy, whose head no one ever stroked.

Bighead slept so close in my tent that truly he was on top of me and each night my arm numbed. Would that cause lasting damage? The first time animal control came they took four: the Little One, Sweet Soft-eyes, Old Baldy, and Beagle-mix. No one else could have said who was missing. Though for days people came by and pressed my hands kindly. One journalist saw the worst: that righteous uniformed bitch wrestling the stick-choke-collar on each one in turn and dragging them to her van, Sweet Soft-eyes sitting back on her hind legs to slow herself, me screaming and screaming until the cops held me back. When the van rolled away the cops just let me go. This journalist walked over, travel pack of tissues in hand.

Did you get all that? I said. Did you see that?

I whistled and the Shining One appeared, returning from the pantry, where people were often good to her. But Bighead, I never saw Bighead again.

# ALICE

*I*t was a good bar, but I was more or less by myself. A woman leaned over the pool table, skin puckering in her breasts. I was reading a book by a writer I used to like, whose novels were said to have galvanized activists in the '70s into revolutionary violence. One such activist, known as a builder of bombs, had mentioned the books several times through the decades, noting that he reread the first one almost every year. Yet he always said almost the same thing about it.

I'd interviewed the writer once, way up in the northeast fishing town where he now lived, but he'd spoken mostly about lobster migration. Despite his success, he'd said, in a tone of too obvious irony, the most money he'd ever made had been from a coffee-table book on funeral parlors. He'd ridden around with a friend early in the '80s, the friend taking photos, him writing. A portrait of American death that had attained cult status and was regularly reprinted. The friend had died shortly after publication, driving drunk. We wrote the whole book driving drunk, he added.

The new book—I was a few chapters in—took place in a frontier town that couldn't be less like the small hills and small harbors where I'd last seen its author. I don't need to be in the West to write about it, he'd said then, in reply to some question of mine, we were on our third pitcher. But now, the book before me in this solicitously dim light, I thought, well, maybe you do.

(Lobsters migrate in queues, he'd told me: single file along the sea floor out into deeper waters. The queues march night and day. Melting arctic ice has disrupted the oceanic current flow and the waters here—he'd waved vaguely—are warming fast. Soon there won't be lobsters here at all, although that may be, as he noted, a minor concern among the disasters rising sea levels will wreak. We don't know why they come and go, he'd said, his fingers in arthritic parade across the table toward my forearm. We still don't know that.)

That evening in the bar I was hoping for a call back from a right-wing radio host, small station, up in one of those forgotten cities on the plains, nearly Canada. Jonathan—of the five the first to be shot, according to forensic experts—had been involved in a refugee resettlement case. An Iraqi who'd worked as an interpreter for his unit had been killed, not in action but executed, as a collaborator. Hundreds died this way; interpreters were pulled away from US military units and killed right there. When the interpreter was shot, the unit he'd served with the longest had made efforts on behalf of his family, to help allow for their resettlement in the States. No small endeavor—the US opened its borders to very few Iraqis, and the application process took years, when it was not threatened with outright shutdown. This northern city was a City of Asylum, as they're called, and one of the soldiers hailed from there, so that's where they started. Petitioning senators and representatives, refugee NGOs, and eventually this radio nutjob had taken up the cause, wanting to give back to those Iraqis who had embraced our war so appropriately that they'd died for their own freedom. Jonathan had written a few letters, offered some sort of recommendation for the wife and kids, and because of his blandly cheerful manner had been the one spoken to by a couple reporters, gone to meet with a senator, then traveled to the northern city itself.

When she lost her husband the wife was thirty-four, the eldest boy thirteen, then a girl, eight, and a boy, five. They'd come to the US once on the radio host's invitation, and posted on his website were photos from a poolside barbeque: him in cargo shorts, the sun in everyone's faces. The widow, in hijab, smiled in the wrong direction. The boy was shirtless and thin, one hand on his sister's shoulder, the other on his brother's damp hair. Around the pool was only concrete, if there was grass you couldn't see it.

On the screen the Donate Now! button was defunct. Last year the family's application had finally been denied.

Where were they now? Returned to Baghdad, fled to Jordan, Syria, fled again? I was determined to find them and determined there would be a story. A story in which Jonathan's murder would be an aside: instead the travails of the refugees, disappeared from middle-class life into this new fate, homeless, paperless, jobless, in the camps or slums, borrowed rooms or rooftops, how many turned to prostitution or left for oil work in the Gulf. I could see the shape of the story: tragic presence of two off-stage murders; quotidian dissolution and humiliation of a family. It was said that in the course of the war four million Iraqis were *displaced*. A word that made me think not of the action of war—tent camps, ethnically cleansed neighborhoods—but water overflowing Archimedes' bathtub: absurd. But this was the verb employed by almost every article, appearing even in the radio host's transcripts, where it stuck out, an interloper among his usual vocabulary. The widow, Samar, had come on his show. Summer, is what he said and how the transcript spelled it. What do you think of America? Like her husband she spoke good English, her replies fluent and banal. I wanted her to say something of the city on the plains. The windmills across the river and in another state towered slim and white, one could run for miles before they would start to near. Whatever she thought of this large-calved wide-voweled man, his voice booming for hours over the flat land and freezing river, she didn't say. Jonathan was in the studio with her, according to the host's introduction, but spoke only once. He was a good man, Jonathan said of the interpreter, I'd have been proud to call him my brother.

The old frontier city survives as only a few blocks, some façades still beautiful, others renovated and insincere. Around them the city extends into suburbs, houses on small lots, veins of highway or state routes along which big-box stores and malls have been planted, each year the frontier of development pushing further south and west. To the east the river flows north, a wild sinusoid, its curves almost laughable. Samar and Jonathan had come in summer, but it had been a bad flood year, and parks and golf courses were still lost to mud, plastic bags and assorted detritus adorned the greening trees. The sandbags were gone, the one washed-out bridge mid-repair. From a map I learned that downtown there was a reconstructed Viking ship, in honor of the city's heritage. Though the pioneers had come by land, of course—no sea had touched this place for more than ten thousand years. The city offered no other tourist destination, no historical sites, seventy miles to the north one Indian museum, that's all. So Samar and the children might have spent an afternoon here, walked slowly around the boat to make the visit last. Where else could they have gone? My phone rang.

I brought the phone to my ear, and on the TV high in the bar's corner a row of local newscasters appeared, hands arranged on the desk in less than natural postures. Cut to a shot of a man in orange, kneeling, head shaved, beside him a figure in black, masked so that only his eyes were, narrowly, revealed. Landscape of sand, periwinkle sky. Was this Syria, was this Iraq? *A message to America*, the screen read, before cutting back to the studio, eliding the video's conclusion, the fate of the kneeling journalist I had wished for days to unsee.

What did you want to know? The voice at my ear was asking, sounding older than its smug public counterpart. Miss?

What do you want to know? the writer had asked me. We stood, not sobering, at the end of a pier, insipid guitar accompanying us from the surf-and-turf place one pier over. The noise drowned out the night birds and the sea pulsed against the barnacled pilings. No, that was later, we'd driven back to his cabin, inland by a lake—it's too light here, he'd said, looking around at the harbor. Let's go to the lake. We sat in his yard, grass damp through my skirt. There were so many stars. These could have been constellations. What do you want to know?

Fish leaped and I listened. Across the lake for no

occasion a firework detonated, a green whistle that briefly arched. That's the sort of thing that interests me, he was saying, and it was then that I realized I hadn't been listening. The crickets had reached a crescendo and though a military base was near we'd neither seen nor heard a single plane.

Just wait, he was saying.

I lay back in the grass.

*I* was sitting on the floor, laptop on lap, starting a new paragraph, when I received a text from Modigliani. *At Xenith's new border outpost*, he wrote, *wish you were here.* Modigliani, who had neither called nor presented himself in weeks, and who when I saw him at a final press conference on the unsolved murders looked at me distantly, heavy eyebrows shifting once. Accusation or reprimand, as this note was: he had said nothing about the outpost nor told me he was going.

*Top 10 places to see before I die*, I wrote back, and turned my phone to silent. I opened my file on Xenith.

The new Xenith operation made its home in a charming southwestern hippy city an hour north of the border. Just the sort of town you'd think might protest the arrival of a private military contractor, but there had been little press about it, and although one-third of the state's residents were Spanish-speaking its anti-immigration policies had become the most draconian in the nation. Xenith had been hired as supplemental border control, not federal, not state, not vigilante, none or all of the above. It was a pilot project, and if it proved successful here other units might be deployed all along the border, augmenting government efforts with their highly trained precision forces, etc. There'd been ripples upon the news getting out, a manageable outcry, ahead it went. Xenith's own statement, which was hard to find, buried in a dull wasteland of PDFs on their website, noted that *last year alone an estimated 400 people died attempting to make the crossing. Xenith is joining the effort to halt this dangerous and illegal practice, which threatens national security and American jobs, as well as the very lives of those who attempt this crime.*

This I texted verbatim to Modigliani, selecting the right emojis.

A few months back twentysome border patrol agents had caught a man crossing illegally and tasered him on the street until his heart stopped. Passersby recorded everything on cell phones, pausing to delete their saved videos and free up memory. The man was hogtied, unarmed, father of five citizens.

Of our five victims, I could still confirm only that Sergei and Jonathan had joined Xenith. Kareem, Diana, Frances—records established they'd spoken with Xenith employees, recruiters, more than once, but I had no payments, no contracts, no firm plans. Yet there were gaps in each record.

Why? I asked each in turn, their faces blurring. The money. The only job they knew. Kareem, I said, why you, Kareem? But why did I hope differently for him—because we had once read of the same atrocity? What did he think would have prevented the death of Farzad Ahmad Muhammad? What did he think one could learn from a death?

There were other PMCs they could have joined, PMCs with different records. In Iraq the three murdered journalists were only the first incident. The second got Xenith kicked out of the country. Unprovoked Xenith men opened fire on a traffic circle: seventeen civilians dead.

But now, I thought, sign with them and you could

work stateside. A step behind or ahead of border patrol, maybe of ICE. Visit the dreams of the children of the undocumented.

*On the outskirts of the city*, the story could begin. *A newcomer has staked his claim*—pathetic. I didn't even know what the Xenith office looked like. The second story of some adobe storefront, the other tenants lawyers and marriage counselors? Down the street the market would assemble once a week, turquoise jewelry, tie-dye as you saw it nowhere anymore, a stationary bike you could ride to blend your own smoothie, handmade leather wallets, tamales, solar energy pamphlets, sandalwood beads, every kind of incense. Xenith men would stroll through like anyone, amid tan women and tart fresh lemonade, babies in strollers wearing baby straw hats. They'd drive south through the desert to work, not to the closest crossing, wretched with tourists and children clamoring to sell any and everything, but out where no one lived and coyotes led groups across at night, people growing thirstier, some bearing drugs, paying whatever price. The Xenith men must have trained: imagine them, departing the flat plateau of the city for the mountains on each horizon, the red-tinged sand too vivid to picture, the rocks like no rocks you know, everywhere cactuses flowering. They'd move swift and silent through the landscape, hills and rock outcrops their cover. In the open desert, where every animal's rustle or night call rang out, it would be harder to hide but easier to spot the small band of those whom they pursued. I see them, Sergei and Jonathan, flitting across the expanse, whatever sort of camo might suit in those gaudy hills, and on a further crest stands Modigliani. He knows their tactics, their weapons. He smells of sunscreen and keeps his bandana damp. He calls to them, he knows them by name. Or he watches from a distance, unacknowledged, unseen. When he looks back over his shoulder he's not looking for me.

I would keep writing each story, though I could almost see where I had gone wrong. I'd thought of the dead more than the killers. The two whose faces I had never known and may never. The seven shots with which they dispatched those five souls. The Qur'an was Kareem's, we believe, what subterfuge it was to destroy it, its pages like leaves to cover the body, as though to rehearse its descent into earth. I believe he was holding it when you came upon him, with the shock of the bullet he wrenched its spine, its pages took to the violated air. The two of you paused by the window to remove the dust coverings from your shoes, then were outside and across the lawn, startled only by that one car, which braked for you, well trained by the deer in this region. I don't know what you would think of me, a woman who has waited so long to be seen by you. I don't know what words we would choose to speak.

Modigliani, what can I say? I look at photographs and write little. My apartment smells of banana, which I have investigated and cannot account for. I go on long walks through what others would call bad neighborhoods. I've learned that the men who live under the nearest bridge are all sex offenders: they can't live on most streets because they must maintain a distance from every school or park or playground, an almost impossible geometry. Boys on corners catcall or ignore me and go on with their business. On certain blocks where I walk I am the only white person I could see, if I could see myself, but this is not interesting enough to start a conversation, and I speak to few people, and other than panhandlers and junkies few speak to me. No one concerns themselves with me, including or especially Modigliani.

I lost a week or two reading about a suicide, official reports pending, a man whose unit was stationed at a base in Afghanistan at the same time as Sergei. One night the man slipped out of bed and took his rifle to the guardhouse, which is where he was found. The incident was receiving attention because it came out that he had been hazed violently for months, and with unpleasant racial overtones, more than overtones. At the time of his death his back still bore the marks of one night's dragging across the floor, he'd had to do pull-ups and push-ups ceaselessly with his mouth full of water, allowed neither to spit nor swallow, his comrades-in-arms close around him, shouting. They had made him speak in his parents' language, which none of them understood, while they jeered. His letters home revealed nothing. But now that he was dead there was the testimony of other soldiers; eight of the men in his unit had been charged.

Sergei might have once stood in line behind this man—this kid—waiting for a meal or a shower. Both men were on the small side, though whether that would incline them to conversation I couldn't say. To pass the time Sergei might make a joke, the kid would laugh. He was so funny, a comrade of Sergei's had told me, chuckling in recollection. A real practical joker, he'd said—but not like you're thinking, I mean, you wouldn't believe the things he pulled off.

Back on base the kid would turn to Sergei, smiling, to ask something, but since I don't know what he might have wondered the scene fades out. And why conjure the dead for the least of their memories? Who may speak of the memories of the dead?

I should leave, I thought again, poking through the trash with my foot, another hunt for the phantom banana. I should follow Modigliani to the Southwest, I should write about Xenith, not just a piece, but a book, the book we all needed. I had the beginning. More than a beginning.

I would go. I would say nothing to him, and maybe then we'd be even.

I had a lover who lived somewhere near where Modigliani was now, a man who had once been a lover. Back then we'd both lived in the city, I was a bundle of internships, he was plotting his escape from grad school: he'd head back home to where he'd grown up (though his people were from the East), work one of the farms, get into the local irrigation council, a traditional set-up run for centuries and mostly in Spanish, which he didn't yet speak. How do you know they'll want you? I asked and he never worried. In time he left and once I went out to visit him, though I remember little; in the mornings the room was cool until the sun hit and it was never cool again. He'd gotten work on an organic pecan farm. He was going to run for a position on the council he'd spoken of, head of the canal diggers, I forget the title, though the word was beautiful. I'm going to write a book about it, he said, and either aloud or silently I condemned him, how could he know before beginning what the book was about? He was not the only white man working the ditches, but one of them. He had gotten thinner. I suspected he had a girlfriend out there that he just avoided the week I visited, and neither of us were concerned, maybe she wasn't either. I would leave soon enough. Did he ever wish otherwise? Once in the middle of the night I had stolen to the bathroom naked and on the way back had to hide under the kitchen table from his roommate, come home unexpectedly. I don't know that I even told him this, we could have laughed about it. And now we never speak, though I believe he lives in the same place, something like the same life.

The reporter was here to watch them build the wall, he said. But he showed up at the zoo every day. Every day I waved him through.

No, no, he said, fingering the coins in his palm, his lips moving as he counted the currency.

The animals are dying, I said, this is not a business.

He'd drift left or right. Bat house or reptile kingdom. The path was, ultimately, a circle.

Do you want to ask me about the wall? I said finally. Two weeks had gone by and he hadn't mentioned it.

What do you want to talk about? he said, sounding surprised, his surprise resembling happiness.

Come, I said, and when we were in front of the buzzards I pointed: it will cross just beyond here. All the birds will be in shadow.

Can they live in shadow? he said.

We'll see, I said.

I had called the bird woman many times, but she no longer answered. She had emigrated a few months, no, a year ago. No one had missed her while Ephraim still lived. Most days you could find Ephraim standing by the cage of the scavengers, whistling, tickling a red wattle, his coveralls foul. The only lover of vultures, I said one day as I approached him, the bucket in my hands heavy and rank. He turned toward me, smiling, and the bird nearest him lurched, blood everywhere. The blood was mine. The birds were shrill but Ephraim was quick, sliding my finger into his mouth. My pinky nail has never grown back.

I'm not carrion, I said then to Ephraim, as if I could win the argument.

He only nodded, his tongue tight over the throb of the wound.

It was Ephraim who guided us when the air raids began. The bat house, he said, and we followed him, descending the stairs. Below ground the sirens seemed no quieter, bats frantic against the glass. They'll take out our eyes, I said.

Close your eyes, said Ephraim.

Wings hit and hit.



I took the reporter past the cage of the lioness, walking very fast. These days she paced very fast. I think it was there that I realized he did not know the word *wall*. He knew the word for it in his own language but not the word we all used. I don't know where our word came from, it was a strange one, but it's what everyone said, from the day we learned the wall would divide our city. When I said this word to the reporter, raising my voice as the lioness brushed against the bars, her fur in the wrong direction, her nearly see-through skin, when I said this word he did not seem to recognize it. He did not seem to know how to respond. What had he been talking to people about? I wondered. What had he believed they were saying?

Come, I said, and I don't know why this was when I took his hand, took him to the tree above the snow leopard's cage. In the twilight the snow leopard got whiter and whiter. If I dropped a leaf through the webbing her tail lashed again. The reporter and I made love there, in the crook, uncomfortably, doing a lot of work with our hands.

She hardly moves, he said of the snow leopard. She lay in the dark, not quite sleeping.

She is probably dying, I said. Or at least, she is starving.

It would be kinder just to kill her, he said.

Almost everyone says that, I said. I slid my flawed pinky into my mouth, a new habit.

Ephraim had died just before the construction of the wall began, the air raids had found him in a Walmart parking lot. He'd been shopping to feed the snakes, whom he hated. I was the one who found him, I went to look when he failed to answer his phone. He looked small where he lay, and there was little blood. The live mice he'd bought had survived, it seemed, they were everywhere, one nestling into the pocket of his shorts, I removed it with a murmur. You don't know what he had planned for you, I said. I carried Ephraim myself, I brought his body back with me. The mice, I thought, too late. On my watch the snakes starved.

The reporter came early in the mornings now and walked the circle beside me. He photographed each empty cage.

Would you like me to make them look more poignant? I said.

How? he said, surprise transforming him.

No, no, I said, I can't, that was the point.

You were making a joke, he said, trying to decipher the placard about the zebra's natural habitat.

We stopped a while by the lioness. He put his phone away.

I said: You're not great with languages.

No, he said.

It's worse than that, he added. I didn't study it. It's a long story but I didn't think I'd end up on your side of the city.

You won't, I said.

What? he said. Then he nodded. She likes you, he said, meaning the lioness. Even though he was there she was licking my forearm with her dry tongue.

She likes salt, I said, and she knows I like her.

She is named for you, he said.

No, I said, it is a very common name. You just only know the two of us.

Later, days later, when we passed what had been the rhinoceros cage, he said, as if he had been waiting to say it: There was a rumor they were used. In the battle before construction began. Led charging into the fight. But they couldn't distinguish between sides, people say, so it was a bloodbath.

Yes, I said quietly, none of them survived.

Don't tell me that's true, he said. That didn't happen.

Everything you've heard is true, I said. I said it in the language he should have known.

In the end he was the one I told about Ephraim's body. What I'd done with it, whose cage I'd brought it to, what I had chosen to hear. It was not that I thought he would understand.

# MARTIN

*T*he epiphany came in the midst of shooting, so suddenly that I ruined a take.

We were filming the penultimate episode in the fifth season. The murder had taken place in some sort of illicit pet depot, imports from South America, that sort of thing. I'd wanted to work with the animals, but in the end I had nothing to do with them, in the shot in which I caress a pale cockatoo breast the hand isn't mine, belongs to some bird trainer, who seemed terrified to meet me, a phenomenon I've come truly to hate. I solved the crime too quickly, through some information that only I had and the audience couldn't know about, dark backstory offered at the end kind of thing. I used to call bullshit on that move but I don't anymore. People want you to know things, I get told, that's your character. You're riding the crest of a wave, secrets in its belly and you toss up the best of them. Detective Garsin, he comes and goes behind civilization's shining façade. You know?

I know.

The show used to be great, is the problem. The detective was based on a real detective, or investigator of some kind, I was never clear on that. He had solved the murder that had brought down an entire software company—a kid had ended up dead for knowing too much, that had actually happened. The show's first season was all stuff like that: political intrigue, one murder, no, I guess two, but a long slow gorgeous plot that spanned the whole twelve episodes, took down a clutch of white collars, a state senator, ended a whole internet spyware kind of deal, none of it predictable, no Manichean bullshit and square-jawed heroes, everything was a little fucked. It was an event, a real television event. But by season four it was a murder every episode, run-of-the-mill cop show and I was just some pale long-faced Columbo who crimesolved by means of his rarefied and highly convenient knowledge of the world's dissolution.

The first and second seasons had gotten buzz like you wouldn't believe and deservedly. By season three things had settled down, the show wasn't so hot anymore, disappointing, but as a bonus it wasn't so bad for me with the tabloids. A few hopefuls still might get their shots as I walked in and out of my apartment or restaurants downtown, but that was it, and I had the best windows and blinds ever manufactured, no light in, no sounds out, you could fuck every which way all day long and the five guys perched in your hedge would know nothing.

But in the middle of season four, no warning, the shitshow was back on. One rag got on a real plastic surgery kick, a so-called series, before and after pictures, exposing who'd had what done, etc. As though you couldn't have known just by looking. We could all learn a few things here, I said to Emilia, how to make some real money. You print celeb shots all day every day, photoshop every face and bikini bod into complete fantasy, so that the actual owners of the faces have to kill themselves just to keep up, and then when things are slow you run an exposé on how they're all phonies, how many times they've gone under the knife. And you charge people who actually work for a living for the privilege of this information.

Emilia doesn't usually warm to such outbursts, maybe a little murmur, a little shake of the head, but it must have been only a week later that she'd called me to say: Babe, I'm so sorry.

It's fine, I said.

Fine? she said. Fine?

What are we talking about, I said, and she said, Oh hon, they've printed your medical records.

And that's what they'd fucking done. *Clues to Detective Garsin's Mystery Disease!* splashed across the cover. And then, indeed, the article was full of references to my medical history, doctors' names, appointment dates, bloodwork ordered, the whole thing, up to each dodgy mole. Luckily it seemed my bout of the clap was too far back to surface. *These records would appear to dispel the rumors of illness that have been dogging the actor...*

Rumors? I asked anyone.

The thing is, Emilia said, they've been saying you've been looking very pale, really sick.

I'm 51 years old, I said, and most of those years were not pretty.

But I knew that wasn't the reason. The reason was Modigliani—that is, the real detective, the one I was based on. My role was based on, that is, Garsin. I'd met the man: when we were shooting the first season he'd come by. Stood in the back, this tall guy in a slouchy leather jacket that was the prototype for the one I wore. Mine in fact fit much better, though I'd always called it ill-fitting, as did the reviews. He was white, really white, a gleam to the forearms his jacket was pushed up to expose. I had a photo of us, one of a few taken around the set, although these had nearly been confiscated by Modigliani. Can't have pictures of me out there, he said, you understand, and they'd had to promise him they'd deleted the files, then offered the three extant prints to the showrunner, Modigliani, and me. I kept mine on the mantle, which amused me. And maybe it's true that as the show went to shit, out of some kind of respect for what once had been I'd stayed devoted to maintaining his appearance.

And although I said nothing of this to anyone, there in the paper, part two of the same goddamn exposé: next to the photo of me, a photo of none other than Modigliani. *Plastic Surgery to Look Like Real-Life Detective?!* the headline inquired. My God, Emilia said. More medical records, this time including a couple scanned pages, printed right there. *The* Post *could find no records of surgery*, the article, if it could be called that, concluded. *And yet rumors continue to circulate, speculating on how actor Woodruff has come to look so much like the real-life sleuth. Friends and costars wonder about his stability. "It's like he's mistaken himself for a real detective," one costar told us—off the record so as not to provoke Woodruff's notorious bad temper.*

Months of legal bullshit later all I got for my troubles was a paragraph acknowledging an error, expressed so vaguely that no one—even those sad souls who read correction boxes—could know what it meant.

You do look like him, actually, my lawyer had said, the photos spread out across his desk. Although, and I'm not just paid to say this, you are significantly better looking.

I am a professional, I said.

That's how it got going between me and the *Post*. After that article I dedicated myself to the papers, read every one. Every Sunday I'd trot myself to the stand on the corner and get the rags and the classics, I'd sit and read all the A sections and check out the rest nice and slow. Impressive, Emilia said. Meaning she was doubtful. I'm reaching a dignified middle age, I told her.

So when some actress won that first lawsuit against the *Post*, I took note. Little druggy brunette who liked married men, but was a real talent. (Emilia said, don't be like that, it was just the one married man and they dated forever. I didn't invent the world, I said back, which I admit is something an asshole would say.) The paper had been hacking into her voicemails, listening to everything and printing all sorts of smutty "quotes," complete with dramatic ellipses. It was unbelievable, but there it was, printed up in paragraphs like anything. They'd admitted to it, in a limited way—one rogue PI, not even on our staff, now fired, they said—and she'd won the suit. And over the next few months a few more suits were filed, first- and second-tier celebrities, same deal. Voicemails hacked.

It had never been my habit to pay attention to things like the news, and I found the experience—the fact that I knew this was happening almost as it happened—an uncomfortable pleasure. I'd always just checked out the front pages of those garbage-bin liners, the lurid snaps: skin-and-bones crooner tottling out of rehab, a reality show bimbo's perp walk, another's suicide note, this or that politician in a dim restaurant with his mistress, this Olympian with his bong, or me, undeniable spring in my step as I strolled out of that gay club one night, having met T there, old habits die hard.

And so there I was, shooting the end of the fifth season, and it came to me: Why not play detective?

I started a file of articles on the hacking, noted reporters' names. I dug around in archives. Sent Emilia to the library. At night online I read up on recording devices, ordered a few. Just in case.

My lawsuit must have gotten me on some list, and the first few reporters I called didn't bite. But then I found Chuck. I'd looked into Chuck and all along I'd thought he could be my man. I didn't call him straight up; I was learning. I rented a car, nice dark windows, started tailing him. I wanted to see what any of them were up to, I wanted to see the whole life. Chuck was a young, nervous type, I think he was South Asian, if that matters. Rumor had it that he'd leaked extra info to the opposition in the hacking suits, out of some on-the-buzzer shot at journalistic ethics. I'd gotten that much from encounters with brunette and her lawyers, as well as reading between the lines of the articles, which made it seem like there'd been a pretty half-hearted instance of whistleblowing. On the sixth day of my tail, Chuck pulled over, got out of his car and started swearing, popped his hood and stared at the engine, but it was just a pose for passing cars, guy looks at engine, he didn't touch a thing. Fuck it, I thought, and pulled over. Need a jump? I said. No way, he said, on seeing me. We didn't talk much, but got the car started.

I owe you one, man, he said.

I take cash, I said, and to acknowledge his debt he acted like that was a joke.

Two nights later I followed Chuck to his favorite

hangout. I was prepared. The word's always been that I'm a total fucking psycho when I lose my temper, and if needed I could call up the old gleam in the eye. There is no man alive who isn't scared of your chest hair, a costume girl had once said to me, unbuttoning one more button and awkwardly fluffing the thatch beneath. Tonight I did the same, for good measure. I went in. Chuck, I said, buying him the beer I'd seen him with the last time. Chuck, how's it going?

Close up, in the light, Chuck was neither young nor nervous. He nodded thanks for the beer. I'm ditching the Honda, he said.

Sometimes you get what you pay for, I said.

Supposed to be the most reliable in the world, he said. I've been brand faithful for a decade, but now—he shrugged—I'm telling you, the future is wide open.

I just up and asked him about the medical records, who had got them, how. If he'd needed more incentive I was ready to give him a little industry dirt I'd stored up, maybe dish on some big names who show up to fuck where you wouldn't expect, there were one or two who could stand a rough week. At first he didn't say much, but then he said enough. In the end it was like he'd been waiting for someone to ask.

Late that night I pulled off the wire, with it some of my luxuriant chest hair, and burned the conversation onto my computer, burned backups as well. Everyone knows, he said, and of course we pay cops. We pay rehab people, doctor's receptionists, how could we get where we do as fast as we do if we didn't?

And the voicemail? I asked.

You just pay your way, he said. And you're in.

Hey, I'm sorry about the medical thing, he said later, drunk but not unconvincing.

Oh, I said, I think I'm going to be all right.


I gave my recording to the cops, but nothing happened. By now it was mid-sixth season and there wouldn't be a seventh. I'd signed up for a raunchy rom-com and a TV miniseries, ripped from the headlines thing, on domestic abuse. Good for you, my agent said, or was it Emilia. I waited three months on the cops: nothing. There's an ongoing investigation, they said, the one time someone worthwhile called me back. But I was busy, we were filming the series finale, which included some post-hurricane scenes that took forever. Once you sank in, if you really just let yourself be in it, it was scary as fuck. The last five episodes had a continuous storyline—my idea. If they've stuck with Garsin this long, I said, give them some of the old magic. The plot was too sensational—some modern-day KKK thing that would let everybody feel good about not being racists, but didn't measure up to what had actually gone down in that city before, during, or after the storm. But who am I to complain, slamming cuffs on a grandmaster, punching one of his redneck minions across the table, classic, cracking the two-way mirror? You look like shit, Emilia said over Skype, and I said: I'm supposed to be living in a trailer with no running water, how good should I look? They'd finally agreed to let me grow some stubble. Small victories.

And so at the end of all this, there I was, looking at my reflection, and I did look gaunter, leaner, unlike myself.

Fuck the police, I thought, I'll go to the papers.

I called one of the women who'd been covering the hacking stories, written what I'd thought were a few nice pieces, nice as far as I was a judge. I have this recording, I said. She was interested. Let's meet in person, I said. She smiled coolly, her blouse crisp but tucked into an ancient jean skirt, acid-washed. She listened, but really she wanted the recording.

I'm a fan, she said, smiling, as she got up to go.

It was nothing, I said, just a night's work, least I could do.

She looked confused and I figured it out, waved a hand.



Who are you anyway, Alice? Later that night I dug in, searched the reporter's name. It was only then that I learned the hurricane shootings—*my* hurricane shootings, I thought, my series finale—had been a real case. Never solved. My girl Alice had written a magazine series on it, hard-hitting, outraged. But they never got the guys. She laid out scene after scene and then, pfff. What. As far as I could tell there were two main candidates for the killers— this private company Xenith or some local racist militia. Except of course the latter might include some cops, which would be one more reason no one had cracked down, no one had gone to jail, other than the sort of people who were always going to jail. Photos of the real-life victims, a man and a woman, loaded slowly on every page I scrolled through. Experts thought they'd died execution-style, on their knees. Obviously whoever'd written this season of Detective Garsin—I should know exactly who—had chosen the militia option, left Xenith out of it. But reading the story I thought they'd chosen wrong. What about this night here, when, according to Alice, the Xenith guys said they'd been shot at by some quote *black gangbangers* near an overpass. *I dropped my phone and returned fire.* There was no end even to that story, just one Xenith kid later saying that afterward *all I heard was moaning and screaming, and the shooting stopped. That was it. Enough said.* Alice never found the gangbangers. There was no report. Cops didn't bestir themselves. To fare well in a situation like this, I thought, you either want to be with Xenith or with Detective Garsin.

And the head of the hurricane investigation—was I even surprised—was none other than Modigliani.

Small world.

To scratch an itch I searched the name Bill LeRoy.

I went to bed.


I could never have called it the way it played out.

The *Post*'s sins caught up with it a pleasant June day a summer later. I still kept up on the news, but not with the same vigor, I wasn't up to much. The rom-com had fallen through and the domestic abuse thing took about ten days, start to finish. I wasn't playing the abuser like I would have in the old days, now I got to be the valiant co-worker. Thank you, Garsin. Left to my own devices I was looking into investing in this community garden thing just north of downtown, buying up the lot next to the garden, which would be good for development if the revitalization took off.

Then, one day on the front page: bam. The face of that girl, the one who'd gone missing and turned up dead almost a decade ago. It was strange to see her again, you kept thinking: shouldn't she be all grown up? I'd been drinking a lot back then, and whenever I'd bobbed to the surface for a few hours, her face was on some screen. Missing two months before they found the body. Jesus, Emilia said, when the girl's face smiled up at her from the paper I held. I thought they caught that guy, she said, I don't want to hear about that ever again.

But this was something new: My little miss reporter had proved the *Post* had hacked the girl's voicemail in the months before she'd turned up dead. Reporters sat around listening to every sobbing desperate message from parents and friends, used any and everything juicy. To keep the story going they deleted messages they were done with, cleared the mailbox. But this of course let everyone—cops, parents, friends, other papers—think maybe the girl was still alive, checking her phone, maybe they could still find her. When she'd been a corpse, gagged, bound, and discarded in a warehouse basement, within a day of going missing. Little miss's story showed up first in one midsized paper, then everywhere. It wasn't the first or last phone hack, maybe not even, all told, the worst—they'd hacked victims of terrorism, former heads of state—but people were calling for blood. And a few articles later, my phone was ringing: *The actor Martin Woodruff, best known for the critically acclaimed but controversially violent series* Detective Garsin, *wore a wire to obtain... A little undercover work of his own...*

I went on the talk shows. I'd filled out a little, in a good way. I said more than I expected. Disgusting, I said. Violation of privacy, of basic ethics, of the public's trust. It surprised me that people kept listening, kept plopping me down in a wheelie chair to say some more. You know, no one's really asked me about anything real before, I said, in response to some question about the appropriate legislative response, and I hadn't finished but there was laughter everywhere, and that line took off, like it was even a line.

Of course it meant I was back to the limelight, cameras and microphones tripping over themselves to get at me. But a higher-class crowd was calling, and no one mentioned the male escort credit card charges from back when, which was polite. New scripts came in.

Well played, I thought, flicking the framed photo of me and Modigliani, but I meant only me. A police chief had resigned. A high-level member of the president's PR staff, who'd come to government from the *Post*: out, and under investigation. The newspaper shut its doors. Its owners—who owned maybe a fifth of the world's papers—were called down from their customary pedestals and made to sweat it out in a hearing or two. They lost some millions. I wore it all well, I thought. Emilia had left me, presumably temporarily, for a spiritual retreat. In her absence I fucked less than usual.

In fact, the reporter was the only one. A couple nice nights in a hotel I thought she'd like. But anyway she never wrote a word about me. I checked. She must have handed off my CD, handed off the whole scoop, who knows. There were plenty of stories, though. I was hot, my agent told me relentlessly, now's the time.

*T*hey say when the water rises, each coast will drown, every skyscraper, hotel, retirement community, luxury beach, the cliffs where the rich weekend. Maybe tourists will travel to see the start of the deluge, what will wash away first in the great storms to come. It's hard to mourn, even early in the day, when the water is mindlessly clear and just warm, and on the beach leather-skinned men gather to play a game of pétanque. It's hard not to feel that the sea has waited long enough. I am so pale in this place, I walk down the sand like a foreigner.

A harbinger.

When I was young and lived back east in the city, in the sort of shabby converted factory flat that people would now kill for, I used to walk down what was then an abandoned street, down to the water that divided the city from itself. The nighttime panorama: bridges to the north and south, the different eras of their architecture demarcated by their lit-up forms, by their reflections in dark water, and facing me was the island, frantic with light, highway along its coast traced by passing headlights, black planes of its skyscrapers now silent, to their south endless bar lights and billboards, too far to discern human figures. The nearest bridge was the oldest and the city's great poets had memorialized it in turn. It was built before anyone understood the danger of pressure in the caissons and seventeen men had died planting its pilings, of what we now call the bends. The rocks before me were slimy and thoroughly littered and I walked out on them to the farthest point, where I imagined, young thing that I was, that if anyone had passed by and seen me, or had come down as well to love the water by night, I would have cut a romantic figure against the dark backdrop, the bright blur of the bridges. Bats flew over and maybe in time they knew me by my form. If I wasn't alone I never knew it, I faced the horizon, the water, the scene.

[          ]

What happened was, in the words of the inquiry, grave and shameful. The army has apologized unreservedly to the families and the surviving victims of this shocking episode. And I would like to take the opportunity to repeat that apology today.

What were the instructions to the guards? That is what the investigation that I have indicated has been undertaken is determining.

To the president, Congress, and the American people, I wish I had been able to convey to them the gravity of this before we saw it in the media.

It means having your hands tied behind your back and then simultaneously having them tied to your legs and your ankles and shackled from behind, left on a floor with a bag over my head, and kicked and punched and left there for several hours, only to be interrogated again. The detainees were hit and kicked, causing them to emit groans and other noises. They were played like musical instruments, a practice known as "the choir." If your head wasn't touching the floor or you let it rise up a little they put their boots on the back of your neck and forced it down. Some soldiers have been suspended from operational duty and military service. Certainly since this firestorm has been raging, it's a question that I've given a lot of thought to. There are many who did their duty professionally and we should mention that as well.

The Geneva Conventions apply to all of the individuals there in one way or another. If you allow them to believe at any point they are more than a dog you've lost control of them. Mr. Chairman, members of the committee. I feel terrible about what happened to these detainees. They are human beings. I deeply regret the damage that has been done. First, to the reputation of the honorable men and women of the armed forces, who are courageously and responsibly and professionally defending our freedoms across the globe. They are truly wonderful human beings. And their families and their loved ones can be enormously proud of them.

Their instructions are to, in the case of Iraq, adhere to the Geneva Convention. Let me tell you the measures we're taking. A special forces guy sat there holding a gun to my temple, a 9mm pistol. He said if I made any movement he'd blow my head off. I heard a scuffle, and then some dull thuds behind cell three. Harshing, or conditioning. ERFing. Told to bend over and then felt something shoved up my anus. I don't know what it was but it was very painful. Shown photographs of Donald Duck, Mickey Mouse, Tom and Jerry, Rugrats, Abraham Lincoln, Michael Jackson, Fidel Castro, Che Guevara, Osama bin Laden and famous people from different countries.

When they took him out they hosed the cell down and the water ran red with blood. I was left in a room and strobe lighting was put on and very loud music. It was a dance version of Eminem played repeatedly.

A new category of "manipulative self-injurious behavior" was created.

We need to review our habits and procedures. One of the things we've tried to do since September 11 is to try to get our department to adjust our procedures and processes. I'm seeking a way to provide appropriate compensation to those detainees. There is nothing we can do to automatically restore the trust which was the second casualty. There was malicious damage to US government property. We value human life. We know what the terrorists will do; we know they will try to exploit all that is bad, and try to obscure all that is good. You killed my family in the towers, and now it's time to get you back. We lived because someone made holes with a machine gun, though they were shooting low and still more died from the bullets. We say to the world, we will strive to do our best, as imperfect as it may be.

I felt that my stomach was being ripped out from my body.

The facts are somewhat different than that.

I lost feeling in my hands for the next six months.

There is a timeline up here.

After which they threatened to have me sent to Egypt, to be tortured, to face electric shocks, to have my fingers broken, to be sexually abused, and the like.

I felt that everything I held sacred was being violated, and they must have felt the same.

This culminated, in my opinion, with the deaths of two fellow detainees, at the hands of US military personnel, to which I myself was partially witness.

A barrage of kicks to my head and back followed.

People are running around with digital cameras and taking these unbelievable photographs and then passing them off, against the law, to the media, to our surprise. You can be absolutely certain that these investigations will discover things, as investigations do.

Every time, the overkill amazed me. I was going out of my mind and didn't know what was going on. I was desperate for it to end.

According to the report the soldier believed the journalist had something clenched in one of his fists and was reaching for something on his person with the other hand. Based on the events of the preceding minutes the soldier assessed the actions as those of a suicide bomber who was taking steps to detonate an IED that posed a lethal threat to numerous soldiers in the immediate area. He shot the individual with his M-4, killing him. It was determined that the soldier complied with the laws of armed conflict and rules of engagement and acted reasonably under the circumstances. The journalist was unarmed and spoke English. His brother received two text messages: *I am hiding. Death has come* and *Pray for me if I die.*

# *A*LICE

**W**hat to do, where to go. Someone had been texting me: coordinates, longitude and latitude. It had taken me a few hours to figure out what the numbers were—real locations—and I couldn't decide if that was embarrassing or impressive. Every few days a text came, and each corresponded to a location where Xenith was operating. At least this was what I first believed: a few had described places where I knew Xenith to be and others were sites where other PMCs operated, I'd discovered after some digging, except that they weren't other, but shell companies whose origins and funding traced back to LeRoy. Then there were sites Xenith seemed to have nothing to do with, though there might be an insurgency Xenith would have been glad to fight. It seemed all I could do—I turned up rumors of a CIA-run prison here, new drone base there, or nothing, nothing—was wait. All roads to Rome? I didn't know the number from which the texts were sent, and the sender responded to queries only with another set of coordinates.

I texted *Thanks* or *!*, replies that could be read as earnest or ironic, I thought, or thought this was my intention.

At night I would hold a map in my head, across the screen of my eyelids project the flattened globe (which projection, which of the possible distortions? It's fair to ask) and pin a radiant dot, like the faltering of nerves that scintillates the vision, at each site. These days I was more anxious than I'd been in years. One night Modigliani called, first I'd heard from him in months. Most years of my life have passed without either his presence or any thought of it. I didn't pick up. In my half-sleep I saw the phone glow twice. Hours later I awoke from a dream I couldn't remember but was relieved to be free of, and had to pee, the short walk to the bathroom was long. Naked I sat on the toilet, phone to my ear, and listened to the message from Modigliani.

Alice, he said. Alice. I've just had a dream about you. I was in Abu Dhabi and saw LeRoy in the airport, walking around with a sheet on his head, can you believe it, thugs in wrap-around sunglasses circling him. Still the big boss, on his phone, looking at no one. He's there now, you know, he's got a huge new contract with their government, to help deal with potential protestors, potential pro-democracy movements. So as he's walking through the terminal a cat crosses his path, not a black cat, just a tabby, tail up, on the hunt. He pauses and one of his men trips over it, they all laugh, just a little stumble, but the cat's back is broken, she pulls herself away using only her front paws. LeRoy doesn't laugh and he quiets his men. Outside a plane lands and its wings are shimmering with a sort of flame, blue and faintly orange. We all act as if this was normal.

I walk out toward the plane and a boy is getting off it, you're right behind him. You look tired and the boy is very thin. The plane is small and you are crossing the tarmac to the gate in the wind. Then from around us everywhere there's gunfire. It's not LeRoy's men, I can see this, they're still at the window, behind glass. The gunfire ceases and we're surrounded by the wounded and the dying. I'm lying on the ground and next to me a suitcase has come open, near my face is the tag, written on it the letter S. I've been shot, I realize, and I pull myself toward you using my arms, the pavement wet beneath me. You're crouching low by the boy, who is nearly dead. His stomach is a bloody ruin, intestines thick in it and his hands grasping at them. Clothing has flown everywhere and you're clearing the mess, lifting a pair of women's panties, bright green, off his shoulder. You're singing a little, I don't know the song. I'm sorry, I say, meaning the boy. You look at me and say, *I was hired to write his obituary.* You look past me. With great effort I turn myself over, to face the sky and what had been behind me. Men in camouflage stand in a semicircle. OK, buddy, I say to the one with the youngest face, but I'm interrupted by streams of piss hitting my leg. They think I'm dead. The sun is too bright. The song you were singing is still in my head, but it's annoying, just the same thing over and over. When I wake up I'm covered in sweat, but in my dream the dampness was their piss and my blood.

I'm sorry, Alice, he says, and the final sibilance is swallowed. I can't tell if he's apologizing for this intimacy, or the silence preceding it, or something greater. I'm so frustrated not to know that I hit delete.

It's quiet again, and warm in the bathroom, where the air conditioning doesn't quite penetrate. I get up. I look at myself in the mirror.

I recall that earlier that night I had poured Modigliani a drink. It was a ceremony only the drunk comprehend. *Modigliani, this one's for the killers.* Let's say, I said to no one, you are American. Or not. Let's say the flight was long and unregistered, flight attendants masked. The plane landed in a country that meant nothing to anyone on it. Shall we call it Poland, or Estonia. The prisons there have long histories, but all in other languages. You never sleep and often are naked. Water fills your eyes, nose, mouth, and, you fear, your lungs. You have spoken to the same men forever and yet you are no closer to a future anyone could name. They are no closer to what we might call an epiphany. A victory, a redemption. They are always on the phone. Now they may throw you into a wall or confine you in a cabinet without calling first for permission. One by one the possibilities increase.

If only I knew what to call you. If only I could have called you brother.

If only we could share something that those who watch could not perceive. The glass is dark.

I look at myself in the mirror. In my twenties a doctor told me I had a slight palsy of the eye muscles, which is why my head tilts to the right: at this angle I see more clearly. I'd never noticed this, though upon examination every photograph of me confirmed it. And my whole life, people have said I'm such a good listener—but it's misdirection, that posture, head cocked as though interested. Why won't you hire Muslims? I'd ask LeRoy, catching him as he slipped from his dark-windowed SUV to the gates of his compound. Muslims can't be trusted to kill Muslims, he'd say. Of course he'd already said this, to some other reporter and years ago, but I liked to imagine it was to me.

GABRIELA

We'd been praying for a lawyer but she's who showed up.

Alice, she said, and extended a hand through the bars.

Alice, I said. So, if you cry enough we'll shrink down and just swim ourselves out of prison?

She blinked at me. Incomprehension or the smell.

I was surprised she recognized me from my photo. It had been months since a mirror but I surmised my roots had come in.

No visiting room? she said. I shook my head and pointed, pushed toward the corner. The old bag in the corner looked at me and got up. Behind us that little thing was moaning again, trickle starting again down her leg.

Alice had a high ponytail and three bottles of water, which didn't fit through the bars. Mouths came forward and she tipped the bottles, placed one hand as needed under upturned chins. Was she a saint or some great white plastic-teated cow?

Hand cupped at her hip she showed me a disposable cell phone, just for me. I slipped it into my bra, which had been growing looser, handy for contraband. Through the bars we were close and she tapped the record icon on her phone. Her perfume was too faint to bring a new smell to this place. Beneath each eye was a dark stain of mascara.

You were among the forty-six reporters who wrote a letter to the traffickers, she said, her accent a postcard

225

from a maple syrup farm. She said: The letter protested the recent murders of journalists and requested—requested *guidelines* so that you could know what might be safely published.

A smell arose, with it the sound of shit on shit in the bucket.

I said: I said to the criminals, tell me how to live!

Did you receive any kind of reply?

My wrists threaded through the bars, I showed her my palms: you're looking at it.

She waited.

We expected none, I said in her language. The letter was meant for you, the foreign press, to tell you what it's like now. The gangs send us letters all the time. You know they pin notes up now next to each cache of bodies they dump.

Alice nodded. The light was dim, her eyes blue.

One of us, I said, has already left for the north, where he is now a ghost, no longer a writer. One is dead, a car accident, who knows. One was strangled. One dismembered. I am in jail, out of the frying pan, so I hear.

I said: There was always a man on the corner. I was dyeing my hair a new color each week. When I saw them on the street my blood moved through me. And I have learned to write fiction.

I said: It is not enough.

There is a screen, I said, and if you write it right anyone reading will think, ah, a screen, and know the truth is behind it.

I could have left, I said. I could have crossed the border. I could have lived like the fumes of a lawnmower.

Tell me something, I said. Tell me where you're from.

She looked off as though into the distance, but there was only the cell, whores, thieves, political prisoners, lookouts, a window through which light pulsed the hours.

I'm from all over, she said. But she was a liar.

If I die, I said, you must tell my brother.

I wasn't serious, but I knew she would like to feel important.

She took my hand.

It's Halloween, she said, the day before the day of the dead.

I shrugged.

I bought a ski mask, she said, so I could go as the police.

Behind us I swear that girl was dying.

What I wanted to write about, I said, were the dead girls on the border. But I couldn't find an angle. I have files, I said, I have dozens of files on dozens of girls, all dead.

I know, she said. She said: I've been to your apartment. I'm sorry.

Did you water the plants?

There were no plants, she said. But I read all the mail.

I was tired of her, she moved her fingers in mine, her skin pale and the swell of her hips like a dream in this light.

Bury me, I said, with my face to the south.

I'm sorry, she said.

Are you? I said. In the end the best thing is to die in your own country.

Would you like to give me any notes? she said. I could deliver them.

My notes are my own.

I would like to join those women, I said. There should be an afterlife where we're all in the same room. Kind of like this—I pointed my thumb over my shoulder.

There will be a trial, she said, you have nothing to worry about. You'll get out of here.

That's what I mean, I said.

Will you write about me? I asked her.

If I can find an angle, she said, lifting my putrid fingers to her soft lips.

For the record, I said, I am a natural brunette.

In the end, she said, the best thing is to go on living where you're not wanted.

Her hair was down now and she looked younger and younger.

We'll remember you, she said.

I told her the truth. I said: That's no consolation.

Her tears didn't even make it to the floor.

# ACKNOWLEDGMENTS

Grateful acknowledgment is made to the following journals, in which excerpts of this novel, in earlier versions, appeared: the *Collagist, Consequence, Diagram, Fact-Simile, Fence, LIT, LVNG*, the *Massachusetts Review, Modern Language Studies, Pleiades, Requited, Route 9*, the *Sierra Nevada Review*, the *Spectacle, Western Humanities Review*, and *Whiskey Island*.

⁜

"[     ]" incorporates found text from apologies offered by American and British governmental and military officials in response to detainee abuse scandals, primarily Donald Rumsfeld's statement regarding Abu Ghraib; it also includes excerpts from statements made by former prisoners at Guantanamo, especially the "Tipton Three," and text from reports on or statements about other incidents in the so-called global war on terror.

Some events described in "Mounir" are based on events related in chapter six of Robert Fisk's *The Great War for Civilisation: The Conquest of the Middle East* (Vintage Books, 2005), in particular his quotations from the testimony of Mohamed Salam. This novel as a whole is indebted to Fisk's work.

"Sam" is indebted to Dexter Filkins's "Letter from Islamabad: The Journalist and the Spies," *New Yorker* (19 September 2011).

Among the many sources drawn on, I wish particularly to acknowledge: William Finnegan, "The Kingpins," *New Yorker* (2 July 2012); Alex Gibney's 2007 film *Taxi to the Dark Side*; Charles Glass, "The Warrior Class," *Harper's* (April 2012); Alma Guillermoprieto, "Mexico: Risking Life for Truth," *New York Review of Books* 59, no. 18 (22 November 2012); Margarita Karapanou, *Rien ne va plus* (1991; trans. Karen Emmerich, Clockroot Books, 2009); Jeremy Scahill's extensive reporting on private military contractors and on covert warfare, particularly as featured on *Democracy Now* and in the *Nation*.

✣

Many editors and agents refused this novel, yet its search for a publisher couldn't have ended better. I am grateful to Rebecca Wolff, and to all those whose work sustains *Fence*.

*Strawberry Fields* has benefited from the generosity of great readers. Especial gratitude to Zach Savich, Pam Thompson, Youssef Rakha, Sarah Blackman, Lindsay Turner, Daniel Torday, Peter Dimock, Sam Allingham, Jenn Mar, Caren Beilin, and Karen Emmerich.

After the years the composition and publication of this book required I find myself in a life different from that in which I began. I wish to note the grace through which I have been allowed passage. Thanks are due to many: those named above and others still.